Sugar Ray Leonard

LOTHROP BOOKS BY JAMES HASKINS

Sugar Ray Leonard

Andrew Young: *Man with a Mission*

The Life and Death of Martin Luther King, Jr.

The Story of Stevie Wonder
  (*winner of the Coretta Scott King award*)

Jobs in Business and Office

From Lew Alcindor to Kareem Abdul-Jabber

Babe Ruth and Hank Aaron: *The Home Run Kings*

Bob McAdoo, Superstar

EVERLAST

Sugar Ray Leonard

by JAMES HASKINS

LOTHROP, LEE & SHEPARD BOOKS • NEW YORK

PHOTO CREDITS
Frontispiece, pages 10, 65, 95, 152: courtesy of *The Baltimore Sun*
Pages 35,46: courtesy Eli Attar, Inc.
Page 82: courtesy Wide World Photos
Pages 102,122: United Press International

Library of Congress Cataloging in Publication Data
Haskins, James, (date)
Sugar Ray Leonard.
Includes index.
Summary: Chronicles the amateur and professional boxing career of the
champion from Palmer Park, Maryland.
1. Leonard, Sugar Ray—Juvenile literature. 2. Boxers (Sports)—United States
—Biography—Juvenile literature. [1. Leonard, Sugar Ray. 2. Boxers (Sports)
3. Afro-American—Biography] I. Title.
GV1132.L42H37   796.8'3'0924   [B]   82-15227
ISBN 0-688-01436-4   AACR2

ACKNOWLEDGMENTS

I am grateful for the help of Colonel Hull of the AAU Boxing Commission, Nancy Oppel of the Baltimore *Sun*, Laurel Burns, and Kathy Benson.

Contents

Muhammad Ali revitalized the public's interest in boxing.

1
A MOST UNLIKELY FIGHTER

Until he was 14 years old, Sugar Ray Leonard did not seem to be the type of kid who would ever get interested in boxing. He was shy; he was a loner; he was skinny. Strenuous physical activity was the last thing that interested him. People now say that Sugar Ray Leonard is a born boxer, but if that is so then he was born at the age of 14.

Just like the rest of us, Sugar Ray Leonard was zero years old when he was born on May 17, 1956. He was the fifth child and fourth son of Cicero and Getha Leonard. Since his mother liked the singing of Ray Charles, she named her new baby Ray Charles Leonard and hoped that he would one day be a famous singer, too.

So far, there had not been anyone famous in the family, on either side. Cicero and Getha came from lines of people who worked hard but who could barely make ends meet. When Ray was born they were living in Wilmington, South Carolina, where Cicero Leonard worked in a Coca-Cola plant. He tried to make enough money to feed, house, and clothe his growing family, but he had little hope of being able to do even that, if they stayed in Wilmington. There were not many opportunities for black people in the South in the 1950s, and there was a lot of discrimination. Ray was only four when the family moved northward to Washington, D.C.

In some ways life was better for the Leonards in the nation's capital. There was still racial discrimination, but Cicero and Getha Leonard both managed to get jobs. Mr. Leonard worked from 2 A.M. to 10 A.M. in a produce market, and Mrs. Leonard worked nights as a nursing assistant in a convalescent home.

But housing was more expensive. The elder Leonards and their five children were cramped in their apartment on Avenue L. It was hard for anyone to have any privacy, and there were still two more girls to come, Sandy and Sharon.

Because their parents were so busy, the Leonard children learned early to take care of themselves and not to expect much individual attention. There was great love in the family, but it had to be spread among a lot of people. Ray's sister Linda and his brothers Roy, Kenny, and Roger learned to get attention by being outgoing and mischievous. Ray was the quiet one. His mother never had to worry that he was getting into something he shouldn't be in. Sometimes, she almost forgot he was there.

Ray was quiet at school, too. At first, he was just naturally quiet, but as he grew older he was also quiet because he realized his family was poor. Other kids had new clothes for school. Ray always wore hand-me-downs from Roger, who was three years older. Other kids could afford the dollar everyone was supposed to bring for class field trips, but there was never a dollar to spare in the Leonards's budget, so Ray would stay home. Sometimes there wasn't even lunch money for all the Leonard children. Ray Leonard felt like a nobody, and when he didn't have to go to school he stayed around home reading and rereading comic books.

Sometimes he would tag along after Roger. The two brothers had a nice relationship. Ray looked up to Roger, and Roger felt protective toward Ray. Roger was outgoing, strong, and athletic, a lover of sports. He wasn't afraid to get into street fights. He let it be known that anyone who picked on his younger brother would have to answer to him. Ray was no coward. He wouldn't walk away from a fight, but he was content to live under Roger's protection.

Ray just didn't like fighting. Roger went to a local Boys Club in Washington, D.C., and was in the boxing program there. When Ray was seven or eight he went to the club with Roger and watched him sparring with another boy. Every time Roger got hit, Ray shut his eyes tight. He didn't like to see his brother hit, and he decided he didn't like boxing at all.

Ray Leonard did something besides go to school and read comic books. He was in the choir of his church. He did have a good voice, and his mother encouraged him to sing whenever he could. Ray liked singing. It was just about the only thing he felt he could do well.

In 1967, when Ray was 11, his family moved from Washington, D.C., to Seat Pleasant, Maryland, just outside the capital. A year later they moved again, this time to their own home on Barlowe Road in Palmer Park, another Maryland suburb. It wasn't going to be easy to keep up the mortgage payments on the house, the elder Leonards told their children. There would not be any money for extras. So the move did not make Ray Leonard feel less poor, although he shared the family's pride in having a house of their own.

It didn't help his basic shyness or lack of confidence to be uprooted twice in a short period of time. But the move to Palmer Park did result in one nice thing for Ray Leonard. He met Derrik Holmes there, and Derrik became his closest friend.

Derrik lived in Ray's neighborhood and already had many friends there, so Ray was flattered when Derrik paid attention to him. Derrik was very outgoing, but he did not seem to mind that Ray was quiet and shy. He just started including Ray in his activities, and Ray was eager to be included.

Derrik liked sports and he got Ray to play basketball and go roller skating after school and on weekends. At the urging of Roger and Derrik, Ray even joined the junior high school wrestling team. When he decided he didn't like that, he still felt he should do something in sports, because Derrik did. So he took up cross-country running. When he pulled a thigh muscle at an early meet, the pain was so unbearable that he couldn't go on. Ray was terribly embarrassed. He quit the team after that, much to the consternation of his family and friends.

Ray's father worried about his adjustment. At 13, he was quiet, rarely speaking unless spoken to. He was such a loner. Except for Derrik, he had no close friends, and even Roger, whom he continued to idolize, couldn't get him to play basketball or any other kind of sport very often. It wasn't that he was a bad kid. On the contrary, he never caused his parents any trouble. Occasionally one or another Leonard child would act up at school, but never Ray. Cicero Leonard wished his son *would* act up once in a while—do something to show that he was a normal teenager. He found it hard to relate to his youngest son, and of course it didn't help Ray to have an almost nonexistent relationship with his father.

When Ray and Derrik were 14 years old, a recreation center was built in Palmer Park. The idea behind it was to give the youngsters of the mostly black, working-class area a healthy outlet for their energies. Too many of them loitered on the street corners, took drugs, and engaged in vandalism and petty thievery. The shopping center had become a hangout for bored and restless kids. Drug selling and prostitution flourished there at night. And wherever these businesses take hold, so does petty crime, because the buyers of drugs and sex need a lot more money than the average teenager in such a town ever has. The Parks Department hoped to get the kids interested in clean, wholesome physical activity. It opened the Palmer Park Recreation Center in 1970. Funding provided for a well-equipped gym with a concentration on basketball, which was the favorite sport of Palmer Park youths.

Dave Jacobs was one of the center's first volunteer coaches. He had a deep interest in the young people of his community and a firm conviction that sports was the best way to channel their energies. He credited sports with helping him to avoid the pitfalls of crime and boredom when he was a youngster. He had gotten involved in boxing as a young man and had even won a district Amateur Athletic Union featherweight title in 1949. Then he had turned professional, doing well as a middleweight. When he married and started a family, he decided that he needed a more secure job and a steady income. He had gone to work delivering merchandise for a pharmacy.

Dave Jacobs wanted the new Recreation Center to have a boxing program. The director of the center, Ollie Dunlap, agreed, but they couldn't get any support from the Parks Department, which controlled the funding.

In the early 1970s boxing was not very popular in America. The popularity of the sport has usually depended on a plentiful supply of talented fighters, and promoters willing to spend the money and take the risks involved in staging the big fights. There didn't seem to be many such fighters or promoters around in the early seventies. In the 1920s and 1930s there had been a lot of small boxing clubs in American cities, clubs that served as training grounds for young fighters. There were not many of these clubs around any more. Big-city gyms and recreation centers still had boxing programs, as did many high schools and colleges, but there was much more activity on the amateur than on the professional level.

There were other reasons for boxing's lack of popularity. Back in the 1950s when television was new and a lot of fights were broadcast, boxing was extremely popular. But as different types of television programs were developed, less air time was available for fights. Also, white fighters had all but disappeared, and that was not good for the sport. A fight between a white and a black might not bring out the best humanitarian feelings in people, but at least it generated excitement. Many whites were not interested to watch black fighters compete against one another, and some felt

that boxing had been taken over by blacks. They turned
to football, where there was still little black involve-
ment.

Finally, the general attitude was that boxing was a
brutal sport. It was too closely identified with the un-
derworld. There had been many scandals in boxing
since World War II, charges of fixed fights and fight
promotions controlled by organized crime. The fact
that there was no one international boxing organization
to formulate one standard set of rules for the professional sport did not help.

Until 1920, many countries, and nearly every state
in the United States, had different boxing organizations and rules. This did not present a major problem,
because boxing was primarily an amateur sport. The
problems began to arise when boxing also became a
professional sport. They arose in the United States in
1920 when New York State, where boxing had been
legal since 1896, passed a law that created the New
York State Athletic Commission. A rival organization,
the private National Boxing Association, was also set
up, with a membership of 13 states. The two compet-
ing organizations sometimes recognized different boxers as world champions in the same weight class.

Similar problems arose in other parts of the world,
but because of arguments over voting power it was not
until the early 1960s that any movement was made toward unifying world professional boxing. In 1963, the
World Boxing Council (WBC) was formed. It included
the British, Continental European, North American,
South American, Oriental, Pan Pacific, and African
Boxing Federations. Almost at the same time, the National Boxing Association changed its name to the

World Boxing Association (WBA), but it still has jurisdiction only in the United States. Also, some states belong to the WBC, and some states belong to both the WBA *and* the WBC. Still, the WBA had, and still has, considerable power.

Today, some 20 years later, the WBA and the WBC are still separate organizations that vie jealously with one another for power. But they do follow the same general rules. Eight major weight divisions are universally recognized: flyweight (not over 112 lb.), bantamweight (118 lb.), featherweight (126 lb.), lightweight (135 lb.), welterweight (147 lb.), middleweight (160 lb.), light heavyweight (175 lb.), and heavyweight (any weight over 175 lb.). In addition, three "junior" weight divisions are generally recognized. The junior has nothing to do with age, but refers to boxers who are too heavy for one of the eight major divisions but too light for the next higher division. These divisions are junior lightweight (130 lb.), junior welterweight (140 lbs.), and junior middleweight (154 lb.)

Rules for ring size, length of rounds and bouts, and what constitutes a knockout or a technical knockout are the same in the WBA and the WBC, and as time goes on, more rules are universally recognized. But the existence of two rival "world" boxing organizations continues to hamper professional boxing, and this was certainly the case back in the early 1970s when the lack of unified organization in the pro game just added to the other problems from which boxing suffered.

Not since 1964 had any fighter sparked the imagination of the public and caused promoters to risk all that was necessary to stage a big fight. At that time, a young heavyweight named Cassius Clay took the crown from Charles "Sonny" Liston. Clay was an exceptionally talented boxer who moved much more quickly than the average heavyweight. More important, he was handsome and had a natural "media personality." Sportswriters loved to quote such unabashed pronouncements as "I'm the greatest." His funny poems also made good copy—"Float like a butterfly, sting like a bee . . ." But Clay converted to the Nation of Islam's version of the Muslim religion and changed his name to Muhammad Ali. That caused him to be criticized by a lot of people who regarded the Nation of Islam as a black racist organization. And when Ali, citing the beliefs of his religion, refused to be inducted into the Army in 1967, he was stripped of his heavyweight title by the WBA *and* WBC. In 1970, he announced he was making a comeback and in 1971 met Joe Frazier, the world heavyweight champion. But Ali's three years of inactivity showed, and he lost to Frazier by decision of the judges and the referee. Most people thought Ali was a has-been. And no other fighter had the charisma needed to bring boxing back to major popularity.

So Dave Jacobs and Ollie Dunlap were turned down when they first requested money and equipment to start a boxing program at the Palmer Park Recreation Center. When they persisted, the Parks Department came through with a small amount of money—barely enough to cover the price of a couple of punching bags. Still, Dave Jacobs was determined to have a boxing program. He got small donations from local merchants to buy boxing gloves. He found an old dresser mirror in a junkyard. His students used it to practice their shadow boxing. He took strips of tape and marked out a "ring" on the Center's basketball court. Because there was no raised canvas ring, only a hard wooden floor, Jacobs told himself that the first thing he had better teach his boxers was *balance.*

One of Jacobs's first students was Derrik Holmes, and so another of his first students was Ray Leonard. At 14, Ray still wasn't much for sports, but Derrik started going to the Recreation Center after school every day. If Ray wanted to be with Derrik he had to go, too. When Jacobs took a look at him, he saw a shy, uncoordinated, skinny kid who didn't seem to have a shred of self-confidence. Ray wouldn't even look Jacobs in the eye. When asked to put on a pair of gloves and strike a boxing pose, Ray put his fists up in the air, copying the poses he'd seen in pictures of boxers who had been famous 50 years before. Jacobs stifled a laugh. This kid was going to need a lot of work.

But in just a few short weeks Jacobs had changed his mind. Ray Leonard was still shy and still skinny, and he still would not look Jacobs in the eye when he spoke or was spoken to, but already his coordination had improved and he seemed to have a natural talent for boxing. Jacobs never had to show him a technique more than once. And what's more, Ray seemed like an entirely different person when he was boxing. He looked his sparring partner squarely in the eye and moved with a confidence that he did not show at other times. In just three or four months he had learned so much that Jacobs told him that, if he stuck with it, he could be a champion one day.

Ray Leonard intended to stick with it. At last he had found something he could do well, and it made an immediate difference in his life. Now he didn't just tag along after Derrik when school was over. He was eager to get to the Recreation Center. Now he was up before five o'clock every morning, waiting at the ballfield behind his house for the other youngsters in the boxing program. They would run together to build up their strength. He found that it was easy to make friends with people you had something in common with. Meanwhile, Derrik Holmes began to lose interest in boxing, and though the two never argued, as time went on they drifted apart.

Although Mrs. Leonard was pleased to see her son so happy and involved, she couldn't get used to the idea that he was boxing. It seemed like the last thing on earth for her son Ray. He was so small and shy, with such a baby face. At least once or twice a week he came home from the Recreation Center with a black eye or a bruised lip. It was all she could do to keep from bursting into tears right in front of him. Seventeen-year-old Roger had been boxing since his Boys Club days. He had suffered his share of bruises over the past seven years, but Roger was tough. He had always been involved in sports and street fights. The hardest thing for Mrs. Leonard to accept was Ray's quitting the church choir when he was 14 1/2. He had done well in the choir, as had two of his sisters. People said he sounded like the rock-and-roll singer Sam Cooke.

The main reason why Ray stopped singing in the choir was that his voice was changing. He was having a hard time controlling the notes that came from his throat, but he was embarrassed to mention this to his mom. Mrs. Leonard's hopes for Ray's singing career were dashed to the ground. It was a long time before she could appreciate her son's explanation, "Mama, I put the singing into swinging."

Nor could Mr. Leonard see his son as a boxer. If it had been any of the boys but Ray, he would have smiled and nodded and talked about his own family's boxing tradition.

Mr. Leonard's father had been a sharecropper in South Carolina—and a man of legendary strength. It was said that he could make a stubborn mule go down on its knees with just one punch. Cicero Leonard inherited his father's strength, and when he was a boy he dreamed of growing up to be just like his boxing idol, Joe Louis, who was a symbol of hope for downtrodden black people across America in the 1930s. After Cicero Leonard joined the Navy he realized part of his dream by boxing as a middleweight in military competitions. Out of 70 fights he lost only 1, and had circumstances been favorable, he might have had a professional career. Instead, like Dave Jacobs, he had married, started a family, and given up his dreams in order to support a wife and children. He was pleased when his son Roger showed an aptitude for boxing and hoped that his old dreams might one day come true for his third son.

But the idea that young Ray was boxing was an idea that Cicero Leonard just could not take seriously. He was aware that he did not know his youngest son very well, for they had never been close. But he thought he had some idea of what one needed to be a good boxer, and he just didn't think Ray had it. He was so convinced of this, in fact, that he paid little attention to Ray's new activity. Cicero Leonard was too busy working, and worrying about paying the mortgage, to waste his time on foolishness.

Ray was saddened by his father's lack of interest, but that did not affect his determination. Dave Jacobs's interest in him spurred his dreams. In many ways, Dave Jacobs became like a second father to Ray. Jacobs was a firm believer in training not just the bodies, but the minds, of his young athletes. He was constantly preaching clean living, faith in God, and the Golden Rule. The youngsters were far more likely to listen to him about these things than to their parents, and Jacobs had considerable influence in the lives of many of the youngsters who frequented the Palmer Park Recreation Center.

Despite the lack of official support and funding, the boxing program at the Center was highly successful. In a matter of a few months Jacobs had boys ready to compete in local amateur contests. To raise money for transportation and entry fees, Mrs. Jacobs would cook cases of chicken and spareribs and make pounds of greens and potato salad, and hold benefit suppers for the boxers. Ollie Dunlap would contact local merchants for donations, and so would Jacobs. They always managed to raise the needed money somehow, and the performance of the Palmer Park kids justified the effort. When they had started the boxing program, Dunlap and Jacobs didn't have any big ideas about turning out great fighters. All they wanted to do was get kids off the streets. But the youngsters did so well in local amateur contests that both men began to realize they had underestimated the boxing talent in Palmer Park. They stepped up their efforts to get the kids involved in amateur competitions.

By the end of 1970 Ray Charles Leonard was boxing in local competitions. One night he asked his father to attend an amateur tournament in which he was fighting. His father was still so skeptical that he agreed with great reluctance—but what he saw that Saturday night removed all doubts from his mind. Ray in the ring was aggressive and confident, and what really struck his father was the change in his facial expression. His eyes were steely, his jaw set—it was a look his father had never seen before. Cicero Leonard was almost speechless. The kid really had something! Why hadn't he known? Mr. Leonard had to admit that he had never bothered to pay much attention to Ray, but after Ray's win that night, he took an active interest in his youngest son's boxing. The relationship between father and son improved greatly.

By the spring of 1971 Ray Leonard had put on 25 pounds, most of it pure muscle. He never shirked his daily roadwork and he was never late for sparring sessions. The "ring" where he sparred was still just four strips of tape on the Recreation Center's basketball court, but as Ray's body developed, so did his skill—by leaps and bounds. Dave Jacobs could not believe how far Ray had progressed in barely a year.

That spring Ray beat Bobby Magruder, who was, according to most, the best amateur boxer in the area. Ray Leonard steamrolled his opponents in regional tournaments. He needed to be challenged, and so Dunlap and Jacobs started thinking nationally.

Even the local competitions in which the kids from the Palmer Park Recreation Center participated were conducted under the auspices of the Amateur Athletic Union of the United States (AAU). This nationwide nonprofit organization sets standards for amateur competitions in most sports. The AAU also sponsored competitions on the national level, and by the latter part of 1971 Ray Leonard was being groomed for the AAU national boxing tournament, and for other national competitions.

One of the great national amateur boxing competitions is the annual Golden Gloves tournament, which was started in 1923 by the Chicago *Tribune.* In 1972 Ray Leonard won the Golden Gloves championship in the lightweight class. Later in the year he reached the quarterfinals in the AAU National Tournament, beating fighters five and ten years older than himself. In fact, Ray was so good that he was allowed to join the 1972 AAU national team that competed against teams from other countries.

It wasn't actually legal for Ray to be on that team. By international amateur athletic rules, the minimum age for international competition was 17. Ray was only 16. But AAU Boxing Chairman Rollie Schwartz decided not to make an issue of Ray's age. He went through the formalities, asking Ray how old he was, but when Ray put on an innocent face and said 17, Schwartz did not question him further. In Schwartz's opinion, the national team needed Ray, no matter how old he was. Schwartz believed that Ray Leonard was the best amateur lightweight boxer in the United States, and when you were playing teams like the Russian national team you needed your best fighters. Besides, the men who were on that AAU national team would get a chance to be in the 1972 Olympics.

Ray Leonard had his first taste of international competition when the Russian amateur boxing team came to Las Vegas, Nevada. His first opponent was a Russian at least six years older and far more experienced. Ray flattened him with a single left hook seconds into the fight. In his next fight, he got knocked down. Ray was up before the count was over, and got his revenge by knocking out his opponent in the third round. After his strong showing against the Russians, Ray was being touted as a sure winner in the 1972 Olympic trials, but his excitement was not so much over winning in Las Vegas as just being there. He had never expected to get a chance to go to that magic city. The experience of flying out to Nevada, seeing the names of the stars on the marquees, and actually seeing comedian Redd Foxx and former welterweight champion Sugar Ray Robinson at ringside were the big thrills for him. Ray discovered, however, that he missed the familiar things of home—his mother's cooking, his own bed, the daily comings and goings of his brothers and sisters. He didn't like living in a dormitory atmosphere with the other U.S. amateur boxers. He was very glad to get back to Palmer Park.

Later that year, in Cincinnati, Ray Leonard lost out in the 1972 Eastern Olympic trials. He lost by decision to a Cincinnatian named Greg Whaley in the semifinals. It was a close and unpopular decision. Many who watched the bout charged that the judges had favored Whaley because he was a native Cincinnatian. They said that Leonard fought the better fight. The decision stood, but in a way no one was the winner. Ray had given Whaley such a beating that he was unable to continue on to the finals of the Olympic trials. In fact, Whaley's boxing career ended with that fight.

For Ray Leonard there was one more chance to

make the 1972 Olympic boxing team. There would be a final "box-off" at Texas Christian University, where teams from the various armed services would compete. If Ray could get on one of those teams, he'd have another shot at the Olympics. After much string pulling, Ray was sent to Texas as a member of the Army team.

He was under a great deal of strain. For a long time he had just been enjoying boxing. Goals like being in the Olympics were fuzzy. They had not meant much to him. But because everyone was so devastated by his loss in Cincinnati, the loss became important to him, too. As he watched Dave Jacobs and others scramble to get him on the Army team, the idea that he ought to be in the Olympics struck him full force. He had one more chance, and he believed that he would be letting everyone who cared about him down, if he muffed it.

He did not want to let them down. He got so worried that he couldn't sleep at night. He lost his appetite and often vomited any food he did eat. But he kept pushing himself. The day before his last-chance fight he was running around a track at Texas Christian University when he collapsed. Dave Jacobs saw his young protégé drop to the ground, and as he ran to him he knew exactly what had happened. The kid was exhausted. He'd had months of constant competition—the Golden Gloves tournament, the AAU National Tournament, the meet against the Russians in Las Vegas, the Eastern Olympic trials in Cincinnati—and all the while the pressure on him to make the Olympic team had built and built. Jacobs could have taken Ray back to the locker room and allowed him to rest for a while, hoping he would feel better. But he cared too much about his young friend. He took Ray to the Army team's doctor, knowing that the doctor would probably disqualify him from the next day's competition.

The doctor did.

The next day Ray insisted that he felt fine. He was angry that his "last chance" had been taken away from him. But Jacobs reminded him that in the end his opportunity to compete in the Olympics would probably have been taken away anyway. He was only 16 and no matter how good a boxer he was, the U.S. Olympic organization would not risk breaking an International Olympics rule when it came to the big competition.

One thing Ray did get out of his association with the national boxing team that year, besides a lot of experience, was a nickname. Watching Ray spar one day before the Eastern Olympic trials, the assistant coach of the U.S. boxing team, Sarge Johnson, remarked to Dave Jacobs, "That kid of yours is sweeter than sugar," and from then on Ray Charles Leonard was known as Sugar Ray.

There was already a legendary boxer named Sugar Ray. Sugar Ray Robinson had held the middleweight title in 1951/52 and from 1955 to 1959. Although he had long since retired, Robinson was still prominent in boxing circles and attended all the major bouts. He had been in Las Vegas to watch the U.S. amateurs compete against the Russian team. But the people who started calling Ray Charles Leonard "Sugar Ray" did not think that Sugar Ray Robinson would mind. Sugar Ray Leonard showed every promise of becoming a champion of equal stature.

2
THE MARCH TO THE OLYMPICS

Boxing did a lot for Sugar Ray Leonard. It gave him a confidence he had never known before. It helped him develop his self-discipline and gave him goals to work for. It gave him the chance to travel to cities he had only dreamed about seeing, and which he managed to appreciate in spite of his homesickness. It also made him popular at school. Fellow students often came up to him and asked about his latest fight. Although he became something of a celebrity in Palmer Park, his basic personality did not change. He was still pretty much a loner, with only a few close friends. But by the time he was 16 he did have a girlfriend.

Juanita Wilkinson was a fellow student at Parkdale High School. She lived right around the corner from Sugar Ray. A small, pretty girl, she was introduced to Ray by one of her girlfriends. He had noticed her long before that.

It took him a while to summon the courage to ask her out. Once he did, they became inseparable. She would go to the Recreation Center to watch him work out after school. They spent nearly every evening together at his house or hers. She went to as many local competitions as she could, but she did not really enjoy them. She hated to see Ray hit, and though he nearly always won his fights he did take his share of punches. Juanita hoped Ray would quit fighting, but she did not try to persuade him to quit. She knew how much boxing meant to him. Since they were too young to get married, all she could do was pray that he did not get hurt before they were old enough to wed. Once they were married and starting a family, she had an idea that Ray would quit boxing of his own accord.

She knew he wasn't going to quit before he had won a gold medal at the 1976 Olympics. That was now a firmly established goal for Sugar Ray Leonard. He really had not thought much about the Olympics until he had lost that fight in Cincinnati. Since then, he had not been able to think about anything else. And when the U.S. team made such a poor showing in Munich, where the 1972 games were held, Sugar Ray began to share the sense of patriotism that many Americans feel about the Olympics. He wanted an Olympic gold medal not just for himself, but also for his country.

Only one U.S. boxer, junior welterweight Ray Seales, won a medal at the games. That was highly embarrassing for U.S. amateur boxing. Officials of the AAU Boxing Commission decided that young boxers in the United States were not being trained correctly. They needed more competitions, especially international competitions. They needed a much better understanding of how boxers in other countries fight.

Sugar Ray Leonard and Dave Jacobs agreed. They would study films of European fighters whenever they could get them. Sugar Ray would fight a foreign opponent whenever he had the chance. And in the meantime he would compete in every local, regional, and national competition, no matter how many bake sales they had to hold to pay the expenses. Sugar Ray Leonard would train as if the 1976 Olympics were four days, rather than four years, away.

In the beginning, Sugar Ray was so fired by his determination to win a gold medal in 1976 that he overexerted himself. He trained too hard, and he competed so often that he hurt his hands. For a fighter, he has rather delicate hands. Fighting several bouts in the space of a few days, as he did when he represented the United States against the Russian and East German teams that year, and when he competed in and won the Golden Gloves tournament, he asked more of them than they could take.

During the Golden Gloves tournament, his hands became swollen and sore. He tried all kinds of remedies, but nothing seemed to work. Dave Jacobs sought to protect Ray's knuckles with padding, but this was not allowed under amateur boxing rules. Only a thin strip of gauze could cover Sugar Ray's knuckles, and that was far short of the protection they needed. So, Ray had to learn to live with the pain. He certainly wasn't going to give up boxing. In spite of the soreness and swelling, he won his bouts. Many people thought his talents were being wasted as an amateur. They thought Sugar Ray Leonard should turn pro.

One of these people was a boxing promoter in Baltimore, Maryland, named Eli Hanover. He sent Eddie Hrica, a well-known boxing "matchmaker" (one who sets up fights between opponents) to talk to Dave Jacobs. Hrica brought along a $5,000 check, made out to Ray, to seal the bargain. But Hrica never got farther in his negotiations than talking briefly with Jacobs, for Jacobs informed him flatly that Sugar Ray was not turning pro. If he turned pro, he could not compete in the Olympics, and Sugar Ray was going to the Olympics.

To Sugar Ray Leonard $5,000 was a lot of money, but he went along with Jacobs's decision because he trusted his judgment, and because winning an Olympic gold medal was the goal that was uppermost in his mind. It might seem strange that a kid who used to have an inferiority complex because he was poor would turn down a chance to make money, but Sugar Ray had learned that when you are really good at something, being poor doesn't matter so much. After all, you can't help the circumstances you are born into, but you can do something about your own, individual circumstances. You can make something of yourself.

Besides, Ray and Jacobs both thought that winning an Olympic championship meant more than just having a gold medal to display. In the past, to other champions, it had meant fame and fortune—big money for the advertising of sports equipment and health foods, personal appearances on television, jobs as "color commentators" for TV sports broadcasts, maybe even a Hollywood film offer. Sugar Ray Leonard wanted his talent to make money for him, just as much as any other athlete does. And he wanted that Olympic gold medal. He was willing to wait for the financial rewards winning it might bring, rather than risk turning pro for $5,000, with no guarantee that he would ever make more than just that in the professional game.

Ray had other reasons for not turning pro. Although he did not know a lot about it, what he did know about the pro game was not encouraging. As a promising young amateur, he had already had his share of visits from has-beens. They were still so tied to the game that they spent most of their time reminiscing about their days in boxing and trying to give advice to newcomers who showed promise. Too often, it seemed to Ray Leonard, these men were alone and unhappy except when they were with other boxers and talking about fighting. And too often all they had to show for their boxing careers were physical injuries—cauliflower ears and broken noses and failed brains. He did not want to end up like them. He was going to use boxing as a stepping stone to better things. He was not going to let boxing use him.

There came a time, from 1973 to 1974, when he was 17 and 18, when Sugar Ray Leonard seriously considered giving up boxing altogether. There were several reasons, all of them perfectly understandable. The first, and probably the most important, was that Juanita became pregnant. On November 22, 1973, she gave birth to their son, Ray, Jr. She had told Sugar Ray that she was pregnant as soon as she had known for sure, and so for months there had been the necessary decisions about what to do and how to do it. With the help of their families, Ray and Juanita had decided that she should go ahead and have the child and that Ray should be its legal father. But it was also decided that Ray and Juanita should not marry, and that was mostly because of Ray. He felt that he could not pursue his march toward the Olympic gold medal if he was married and responsible for a family. Dave Jacobs agreed, and so did his parents. So did Juanita and her father.

Juanita realized that if she tried to force Ray to give

up boxing and become a "responsible family man" at the age of 17, Ray would not stay with her and might also give up boxing before he was ready. She loved him too much to ask him to destroy both his career and his life. In making this decision, she showed great compassion for the man she loved. She compared their dreams and realized they could come true if she did not demand all of her dream at once. Her dream was to be married to Ray and to have his child. She was having his child. If she insisted on also marrying Ray at this time, she would deprive him of his dream of winning the gold medal. If she let him have his dream now, he would be happy to get married later. Meanwhile, after Ray, Jr., was born, Juanita dropped out of high school (she would later make up the work she had missed and graduate). She remained at home with her father, while Ray continued to live at home with his parents.

Sugar Ray Leonard did not like being a father who could not support his son. He did not like the idea that Juanita had taken on the adult responsibility of child rearing while he was still pursuing what, by comparison, seemed a kid's dream. After the birth of Ray, Jr., he began to lose his single-minded determination to win the Olympic gold medal. He began to resent being constantly in training while just about everyone else he knew was leading a normal life. Although his brother Roger was still aiming for excellence in amateur boxing, his closest friends were not in training. They could go to parties and school functions, or just stay up all night watching TV, without feeling guilty.

He had to get up before the sun every morning and run around a ballfield before he went to school. He had to spend every afternoon and evening either catching

The National U.S. Amateur Boxing Team, 1973.
(Sugar Ray, center right.)

up on his homework, sparring and working out, or going to one competition or another. He had to travel to foreign countries, sometimes for a month or longer, and he hated being away from home.

Sugar Ray went overseas for the first time in 1973. He accompanied the U.S. national amateur team on a month-long tour that took him to several countries in Europe and wound up in Russia. Although he fought well, he felt homesick from the start. By the time the team reached Moscow he was feeling downright hopeless. He hated the food and was living entirely on ice cream. He felt uncomfortable among the Russians. More than any other people he had encountered on the trip, the Russians seemed to stare curiously at him. They are taught that the United States is an oppressive country because of the way black people are treated. But Sugar Ray did not realize that the Russian people were curious because they learn so much about discrimination and segregation in the United States. He was terribly depressed and despondent and thought he was going crazy. Fortunately, although he had left the church choir a few years earlier, he had not left the church. He believed that God could help him. He got down on his knees and prayed, and he managed to get through that European trip.

He would also survive future trips abroad, including his 1975 trip to the Pan American Games, but the trips were always ordeals for him.

A number of factors caused Sugar Ray Leonard to lose his fierce determination to go to the 1976 Olympics. That shiny gold medal had become tarnished in his mind, and it is likely that his performance at competitions in 1974 was affected by his mental state.

It is hard to measure the effects of an athlete's mental state in competition. More accurately, it is hard to know just what will affect his or her mental state adversely. There are times when an athlete can be going through the worst possible emotional problems and still perform at peak. There are also times when personal problems seem to hurt athletic performance. Neither the athlete nor the outside observer can pinpoint the effects exactly, but it is probably no coincidence that in the year after his son was born out of wedlock, Sugar Ray Leonard lost some important fights.

At least one of these fights was a clear-cut loss. In the 1974 national AAU finals, Sugar Ray lost to Randy Shields, and there didn't seem to be any politics behind the judges' decision.

Sugar Ray's other losses were against foreign opponents in their own countries, and both losses were highly controversial. Against Russian champion Anatoli Kamnev, Sugar Ray fought so well that when the judges awarded the win to Kamnev, the largely Russian audience booed. Kamnev himself walked across the ring and gave Leonard the trophy he had just won. Still, on the record books it went down as a loss for Sugar Ray. Also in 1974, in Poland, Sugar Ray lost by decision to a Polish fighter, although he actually knocked his opponent down three times in the final round and in the opinion of most observers knocked him out the last time. The Polish referee ruled that Sugar Ray had punched Kazimier Szczerba for the third and final time after the match-ending bell had sounded. Even though Szczerba had to be literally held up by his trainers as he received the victor's trophy, this decision against Leonard also stood in the record books. It was the fifth and last loss of his amateur career.

Such close, "political" losses did not help Ray Leonard's attitude toward boxing, which became worse and worse as 1974 progressed. Many times he came very close to hanging up his gloves, but fortunately he was talked out of it. His brother Roger (who had enlisted in the Air Force and was distinguishing himself in military boxing competition), his father, and everyone at the Palmer Park Recreation Center urged him not to quit. One of his most persistent supporters was Janks Morton, an assistant trainer at the center and a former pro football player. Morton liked Ray, not only as a boxer, but also as a person. He thought it would be tragic for Ray to throw away all the years of strict training and all his considerable talent. Ray respected what Morton had to say and what the others who cared about him said. Gradually, the old determination to win that Olympic gold medal returned, but he promised himself that with the Olympics he would end his boxing career. He wanted to go to college and major in communications. Eventually he wanted a career in television. Through boxing he had learned that he enjoyed being in the spotlight, that there was a lot of "natural ham" in him. People responded to him. They liked him, and this caused Ray to be even more personable when he was in the spotlight. Yes, he definitely wanted a career that would enable him to keep on being there.

So Ray Leonard continued to work, even though the conditions under which he trained were still not good. The Palmer Park Recreation Center had yet to acquire a real boxing ring (and would not until 1976), so when Ray sparred there, he did so inside taped boundaries.

During the summer of 1975 there was a special basketball program at the Center, and Ray's time to train for the annual Pan American Games was severely cut. He'd just get warmed up when Director Ollie Dunlap would sadly inform him and Dave Jacobs that the basketball players needed the whole court, which included the boxing "ring." Nevertheless, Sugar Ray was a champion at the Pan American Games.

By 1975 everyone involved in amateur boxing in the United States was getting excited about the upcoming Olympics. AAU Boxing Commission officials were working energetically to get U.S. boxers into as many international competitions as possible. They were successful. Between the 1972 and the 1976 Olympics, U.S. amateur boxers competed against foreign teams some 50 times, including 33 times overseas. No one boxer competed in more than 10 or 15 matches, and the reason for that was that the AAU officials did not want the foreign teams to know how much talent was around in U.S. amateur boxing. There was a lot of it, thanks to the efforts of the AAU and other amateur boxing organizations. Since the 1972 Olympics, young talent had been encouraged to develop and had been given many opportunities to compete. The 1976 Olympic team was going to be much better than the 1972 team. In fact, it had the potential to be great. In addition to Sugar Ray Leonard it would include two brothers named Leon and Michael Spinks, as well as Howard Davis. Unfortunately, it would not include Roger Leonard.

Roger's best fighting weight was 139 pounds, which put him in the AAU light-welterweight class. That was Sugar Ray's weight, and Roger did not want to compete against his brother in the Olympic trials. So he put on more weight and competed in the next higher, 147-pound welterweight class, where he lost in the semifinals.

By late May 1976 the U.S. Olympic boxing team had been selected, and with his teammates Sugar Ray Leonard traveled to Burlington, Vermont, for a month of intensive training. There, his training was taken over by Olympic team coaches. Dave Jacobs and Janks Morton stayed behind in Palmer Park. And of course so did Juanita and Ray, Jr., and the rest of his family. Being far away in Vermont was not a happy situation for Sugar Ray. A homebody, he had never liked being away for more than a couple of days. When he did have to be away, he called home so often that his mother nearly fainted at the sight of the telephone bills. Now he faced nearly two months of being gone, for after Burlington there was Montreal. Hoping to stave off the homesickness that he knew would come, he armed himself with pictures of his family, including photographs of Juanita and Ray, Jr., in a variety of sizes.

No one but Sugar Ray and his friends and family back home knew that he was homesick. To his teammates and coaches, and to Olympic officials, he seemed quiet but happy and confident—a nice young man who was easy to get along with. The U.S. press found him especially attractive. His boyish face and big smile were photogenic, his on-camera presence was sparkling, and he was completely relaxed during interviews. Soon, he was indeed the "darling" of the American team, the essence of the clean-cut All-American boy. Reporters did not seem to mind that he had a son out of wedlock. Sugar Ray was so matter-of-fact about it and so clearly proud of Juanita and

Ray, Jr., tiny pictures of whom he wore pinned to his boxing socks. Reporters saw no reason to play up this flaw in his otherwise perfect image.

Ray saw competition early in the Olympic games. His first bout took place on the first full day of competition, and he was excused from participating in the long march to open the games by the president of the U.S. team so he could conserve his strength. His opponent in that first match was a Swede named Ulf Carlsson, and Ray took the three-round bout easily, controlling it all the way. It was as if he took the occasion to display every aspect of his crowd-pleasing ring personality, which has been described as a combination of Kid Gavilan, Sugar Ray Robinson, and Muhammad Ali.

Kid Gavilan was a welterweight in the 1940s who was famous for his "bolo" punches: uppercuts that start from behind the body, with the arm wound up as if to throw a baseball. Sugar Ray Robinson was famous in his heyday for his lightning-quick combinations of left and right punches. And of course Muhammad Ali, who had regained his heavyweight title in 1974, is known for a number of unorthodox ring techniques. Probably the most famous is the "Ali Shuffle," in which he danced around the ring with his arms dangling by his sides, always in position to attack or defend. Sugar Ray Leonard used all three of these techniques, combining them with a few of his own, such as flashing a brilliant smile at his opponent after being hit.

At times during the past couple of years he had deliberately not used these tactics. Although he firmly believed that they were effective ways to "psych" opponents, he knew that some people resented them as "hotdogging." This was especially true of foreign judges. After his 1974 losses to the Polish boxer Kazimier Szczerba in Poland and to the Russian Anatoli Kamnev in Moscow, some American boxing officials had told him that he had probably lost both decisions because the Poles and Russians had not taken kindly to his showboating tactics. From then on, Sugar Ray fought "straight up" whenever he was in an unfriendly arena. But in Montreal in 1976, the atmosphere was pro-American, and Sugar Ray decided he was going to fight his natural way. He had worked long and hard to get to Montreal and he was going to quit boxing after the Olympics. He was going to go out in style.

Sugar Ray's next opponent was a Russian named Valery Limasov, an experienced left-hander. But Ray was not embarrassed by the unorthodox style that all left-handed fighters have; he did not lose his timing or his balance. He had no trouble landing his punches, and he landed some *hard* punches. Still, the Russian stayed in the fight for the whole three rounds. Although Sugar Ray was the clear winner almost from the start of the fight, the courage shown by Limasov won him everyone's respect.

Sugar Ray then showed why he was so popular with the press. Right there in the ring he opened and displayed the flag of Prince Georges County, Maryland, where Palmer Park is located. Above the red and white flag, his beaming face grinned right at the television cameras: Sugar Ray Leonard, all-American boy.

Sugar Ray was still a long way from the Olympic gold medal. He would have to face four more opponents, each of whom would already have won their initial Olympic contests, too. His next opponent was an Englishman named Clinton McKenzie, and he, too, was polished off in the third round by Sugar Ray.

Sugar Ray won the fight handily. He had unleashed a flurry of combinations at the end of the first round, landed both solid right jabs and left hooks in the second, and scored with another series of combinations to finish off McKenzie at the end of the third. But he had also feinted, shuffled, smiled, and danced. Many in the crowd were Canadians of English heritage, like McKenzie. And there hadn't been much punching in the bout. An unfamiliar sound rose from the crowd when he did this: boos. At the end, the cheers drowned out the boos, of course, but Ray couldn't help feeling bad about the negative reaction.

Modern boxing is probably the least understood sport. People expect to see opponents pummel each other until one drops. They don't understand the subtle techniques whereby the contestants try to confuse their opponents, mar their timing, and control the match.

Sugar Ray felt a great letdown after each of his Olympic contests. He always felt something of a letdown after a fight because of all the training and self-discipline and "self-psyching" that leads up to one. But as a rule he could then go home to his family and friends. Here in Montreal he could not go home, and telephoning just wasn't the same thing. Because there were so many fighters from so many countries, engaging in so many contests, his bouts were spread out. He had already been in Montreal over a week, and before that there had been the month at Olympic training camp in Vermont.

It was a strange life for the Olympians at Montreal. Back in 1972, at the Olympic games in Munich, Palestinian terrorists had broken into the Olympic Village and several members of the Israeli Olympic team had been killed. To ensure that nothing like that happened in 1976, there was tight security at the Montreal Olympic Village. An army of security guards was always checking identity cards and patrolling. Although Ray understood why, he sometimes felt like a prisoner. It was hard living in dormitories with a bunch of other guys when all he could think about were Juanita and Ray, Jr. As he gazed at his pictures of them, he told himself that if he could just keep himself up mentally —and if his hands would just hold out—all of this would be over in a few days. He would have his gold medal and he could start living a normal life.

His next step was the quarterfinals, where he beat Ulrich Beyer of East Germany without any trouble. Advancing to the semifinals, he learned that his opponent would be none other than Kazimier Szczerba, the man who had beaten him in that disputed decision in a Polish arena back in 1974. He had no trouble psyching himself up for this particular fight, but he realized he had to be careful. His hands, especially his right knuckles, were really bothering him. As usual, ice packs, Epsom Salts, and Ben-Gay were not doing much to relieve the swelling or the pain. So when he met Szczerba he conserved his energy as much as he could. Favoring his right hand, he concentrated on his left jab and hook. Even holding back in this way, he managed to beat Szczerba. In fact, so there would be no opportunity for the decision to go any other way, he knocked Szczerba out.

Sugar Ray called home after his victory, but there was no answer at either Juanita's or his parents' and he felt pretty dejected. Didn't anyone care? Here he was subjecting himself to physical abuse, endangering his hands, and back in Palmer Park people who were supposed to be pulling for him were just going about their business as usual. He had no way of knowing that his loved ones were not at home by the phone because they were on their way to Montreal.

It had been Dave Jacobs's idea. He could have flown up to Montreal himself, but he couldn't leave Ray's family behind without feeling guilty. The Leonards and Juanita certainly couldn't afford air fare to Canada. So, Jacobs decided they would all go, by van. When Jacobs took his idea to the Leonards, they wasted no time. Cicero Leonard's boss at the supermarket would not pay him for the days he was out of work, but Mr. Leonard decided he was going anyway. The opportunity to see his son win an Olympic gold medal was a lot more important than a few days' pay.

The van, which was designed to accommodate six people, held ten: Dave Jacobs; Mr. and Mrs. Leonard; Roger, who was home on leave from the Air Force; Juanita; Ray, Jr.; Ray's two younger sisters, Sharon and Sandy; and two of Ray's friends. They covered the side windows of the van with pictures of Sugar Ray and put a sign on the back that read:

WE'VE COME A LONG WAY TO SEE
SUGAR RAY WIN THE GOLD MEDAL—ALL THE
WAY FROM PALMER PARK, MD.,
PRINCE GEORGES COUNTY, U.S.A.

Then they set off on the 14-hour drive to Montreal. It was a long, tiring, uncomfortable trip. They began to

Two young fighters with coach Dave Jacobs.
(Sugar Ray, right.)

feel like sardines in the van, and Dave Jacobs became known as "King Sardine." But no one did any serious complaining; they were too excited and happy to be going to the Olympics.

The morning after his fight with Szczerba, Ray Leonard was getting ready to go out and run when he looked up to see ten tired but smiling faces. They had driven all night, and taken a couple of wrong turns along the way, but they were there at last. Sugar Ray had never been happier in his life. The men decided to spend the next couple of nights in the van, which was parked in a lot across from the boxing arena. They spent the money for a room in a nearby motel for the women. All spent their days at the van, which became quite an attraction to visitors at the Olympics. Some of these visitors helped them get tickets to Sugar Ray's title fight, and on the night of the big bout his own personal fan club was right there in the VIP section, cheering him on.

Ray's final opponent was a Cuban known for his powerful punches, especially his left hook. His name was Andres Aldama. He had beaten his five earlier opponents even more easily than Sugar Ray had beaten his. Ray's coaches had studied Aldama's fighting style and, knowing that Aldama and his Cuban coaches had also been studying Sugar Ray's, they decided that Ray should change his style. Instead of staying outside, feinting and dancing, he should move inside, denying Aldama the room to unleash his powerful left hook. Sugar Ray agreed, and when the opening bell sounded he went immediately on the attack. Although Aldama refused to give any ground, he was clearly hampered. Sugar Ray kept up his charge and in the second round

Aldama did step back as Ray unleashed one of his light-ning-quick series of punches. Perhaps confused by the blows, about a minute later as the two fighters clutched each other, Aldama thought he saw the referee signal that they break apart. He hesitated only a moment, but it was time enough for Ray to land a solid left hook on his chin and drive Aldama to one knee. The referee had counted eight before the Cuban got up. Now Aldama was worried. He came out in the third round looking for a knockout. But Leonard had the psychological advantage. Easily ducking Aldama's wild punches, he unloaded a five-punch flurry on the Cuban's head and forced him to take a standing eight count, a regulation in boxing requiring that after a knockdown the fight does not continue until a mandatory count of eight has been called. Again Sugar Ray attacked and again Aldama took a standing count. The final bell rang. There was no question about it: in his 150th amateur fight, Sugar Ray Leonard had scored his 145th win. The Olympic gold medal was his!

People were cheering wildly. Howard Cosell, who had been covering the fight at ringside for television, pushed up against Sugar Ray. Cosell had predicted Leonard's popularity at the Olympics even before the games had started. Now he was predicting that Leonard would be a rich and great fighter once he turned professional. But Ray shook his head. "I've fought my last fight," he said. "My journey has ended. My dream is fulfilled."

Strangely, Sugar Ray was not feeling very fulfilled at that moment. He was not feeling anything at all. Almost in a daze, he bent to receive the gold medal around his neck. Then, amid cheers, he walked alone out of the arena. His family and friends looked all over for him. At last they found him, out in the parking lot, sitting in the van. He told them he wanted to go home. He didn't even want to go back to the Olympic Village and pick up his belongings. All he wanted was to go home, and he wanted to go home *now*.

3
SUGAR RAY TURNS PRO

The van got a lot of attention as it made its way back to Palmer Park from Montreal. Though the U.S. Olympic boxing team as a whole had done tremendously well —Leon· and Michael Spinks, among others, had also won gold medals—it was Sugar Ray who had really captured the public's attention. The border guard at the St. Lawrence Seaway wanted to touch the medal— and kiss Sugar Ray's mother! Fellow motorists honked their horns, gas station attendants wanted to shake Ray's hand, and when they reached the outskirts of Palmer Park they found a police escort waiting for them. The whole town had turned out to welcome them home.

For the next few days there was no rest for Sugar Ray Leonard, or for any of his family. The telephone rang constantly. Reporters showed up at all hours for interviews. Photographers kept asking for "just one more picture." County officials came to call; mail from all over the world began to arrive in big cloth bags; friends from high school, the neighborhood, and the Recreation Center dropped by. Everyone kept asking him

50

why he didn't want to turn pro. He had the talent, he had the fame. If he turned pro he could make a lot of money. But Ray's mind was made up. He was going to school. Muhammad Ali, who was still his boxing idol, frequently told young athletes to get an education first, no matter how good they were in sports. The odds were always against a young athlete ever making it in professional sports, but the odds were always on the side of a young person with a good education. Ray had taken that advice to heart. Despite his busy boxing schedule, he had managed to graduate from high school and had been offered a congressional scholarship to the University of Maryland. In another two months, he would be a college student, majoring in communications. He also had plans to do something in the recreational field, so kids like him could have the chance to become somebody through athletics. Meanwhile, of course, he was thinking about all the financial opportunities he expected as a result of his Olympic victory. He could just see his picture on the Wheaties box, and his fantasy of doing something in television or films was almost as clear. Then, just two days after his return home, Sugar Ray was the subject of headlines he had not expected to see. Sugar Ray Leonard, Olympic hero, had been named in a paternity suit!

A paternity suit is a legal charge by a woman that a certain man is the father of her child. Such charges are often made, and sometimes they are true and sometimes they are not. True or not, when the man in question is well known, they make headlines. Usually, a woman makes this charge when the man in question denies that he is the father. The strange thing about this paternity suit was that it had been brought by Juanita

Wilkinson, and that Ray Leonard had never denied he was the father of Ray, Jr.

The suit came about because Juanita had applied for public assistance, without telling Ray or his parents. She knew how hard Ray was training for the Olympics, and she didn't want to upset him. But having a small child is expensive. The doctor's care, food, clothes, shoes, toys, all the other things Little Ray needed were just too much for Juanita and her father to handle alone. Sugar Ray didn't have any money, and his parents were still not in a position to give enough financial help, even though some of their older children were now self-supporting. So, while Ray was in Montreal, Juanita applied for food stamps; she had no idea what would happen as a result.

Since 1975 and the passage of a new Maryland law aimed at curbing welfare cheating, it had been standard procedure to start a paternity suit when an unwed mother applied for public assistance. The suit was required as part of the proof that the woman was eligible for help. Juanita filled out the forms she was told to fill out, but she really did not understand the procedure. She certainly did not expect the newspapers to find out about it. But someone in the welfare department must have leaked the story to the Washington *Star*. The *Star*'s story said that the suit was a formality, necessary whether or not Ray acknowledged being the father. But that part was in small print! What stuck in people's minds was the headline: SUGAR RAY'S PATERNITY SUIT. When Ray saw that headline he was furious. He was mad at Juanita for not telling him that she had applied for welfare, but he was especially mad at the press and the welfare people who had chosen this particular time to make a scandal out of something he regarded as a personal problem, although he had never made any secret of it. All he could think about were the hundreds of kids who looked up to him. What kind of example would he be for them, now that he was known as someone who shirked his responsibilities?

Juanita was so upset she felt as if she wanted to crawl into a hole and never come out. Ray's parents were upset. Everyone was upset, but they managed to get through it. After they had a chance to think about it, the Leonards came to the conclusion that Juanita should have asked them before applying for public assistance. They would have worked something out. Still, Ray and his parents realized that Juanita had meant no harm. She had been in a terrible bind, needing help but not wanting to worry Ray. Ray himself would eventually come to realize that Juanita had borne a far greater share of the burden for Ray, Jr., than he had, and he determined that he would make it up to her somehow.

In general, the public supported Ray. He received plenty of hate mail, but he also received letters from people who thought the Washington *Star* story had been unfair. The *Star* got many such letters, too, and an official of the paper publicly admitted that the story had been oversensationalized. However, the damage had already been done. It is impossible to say how many product-endorsement offers Ray might have gotten, how many chances to make television commercials for big fees, if the paternity suit had never happened. It did happen, and there were no such offers.

There were plenty of other offers—big-sounding schemes that excited Sugar Ray, schemes that promised to make him a lot of money. Whenever he expressed interest, the schemers said they'd get back to him with details. While he waited for these details, he started accepting invitations to appear for free at scores of gyms and recreation centers and schools. He had always been willing to make such appearances, but now it was especially important to him to show young people that he was not a shirker of responsibilities, that by his work and effort during the past four years and more, he did have something to say to young people.

Ray was kept so busy making personal appearances over the next couple of months that he didn't have time to think much about what he was going to do for the rest of his life, and he was glad of that. He was deeply confused. He still wasn't supporting Juanita and his son and didn't know how he could. He didn't think that he could now go off to the University of Maryland and leave her to fend for herself for another four years. He kept waiting for the proposers of all those big schemes to get back to him, but they didn't seem to be in any hurry. He still hadn't been offered any big commercial endorsements and he was beginning to understand, again, one of the realities of his life: He was not Mark Spitz or Bruce Jenner. They were white, like the majority of people who buy any product in America. He was black, and not only was he black, he was an unwed father who had been the subject of a highly publicized paternity suit. Within a month after his return from Montreal he also discovered, to his sad surprise, that people were already forgetting the Olympics.

At the time he was accompanying Janks Morton, whose steady job was selling insurance, on his selling rounds a couple of days a week. They would arrive at a prospective client's and Morton would proudly introduce Sugar Ray Leonard, and the client's face would get a blank look. Ray Leonard began to realize how fleeting fame was. All that hard work had indeed earned him the Olympic gold medal, but that might be all he'd ever get. He did not like to see the spotlight slipping away.

In late September Ray did get an offer that he knew was real. He and Morton were invited to New York as guests of fight promoter Don King to see the heavyweight title bout between Muhammad Ali and Ken Norton. There, King presented him with a big-money offer to turn pro. But the contract King wanted Sugar Ray to sign contained so many options in King's favor that he would practically be owned by King. About the same time Muhammad Ali gave him some advice that was very appropriate: If you decide to turn pro, Ali warned, make sure you don't sign your life away. Do not make the same mistake Ali had made.

There were many other offers for Sugar Ray to turn pro. He couldn't make up his mind. He didn't want to be owned. He didn't even want to be a pro fighter. He couldn't really afford to go to college because the congressional scholarship did not include money for day-to-day living. In the early fall he visited the University of Vermont for a week. He had made some friends there during the month he had trained for the Olympics, and he hoped that getting away from it all would help him sort things out. But it really didn't.

Meanwhile, Janks Morton, for one, was getting worried about Ray's inability to make a decision, especially about whether or not to turn pro. He knew that Sugar Ray's career could be boosted by his Olympic victory for only so long. Already some people didn't seem to recognize his name. Even boxing people would not remain excited about him forever. If he waited too long, he would be a has-been. Right now, he was in top physical condition. His mind and heart, though confused, were still in the habit of focusing determinedly on a goal. If he waited very long, he might lose not just his physical shape but his will and determination to box.

Morton decided that someone had to step in and give Ray some direction. He couldn't be pushed into anything, but someone had to help give Ray a clearer idea of his options, and the consequences of each. Someone had to help bring some order into his life. Morton arranged for Ray to meet with Charles Brotman, a public-relations man. The two got along well, and soon Ray Leonard presented Brotman with a bunch of slips of paper, napkins, restaurant receipts, and so on, on which he had made hasty notes about places he was supposed to visit and business deals he was supposed to be involved in. There was just no order to them.

Brotman's first action was to set up a schedule of appearances that would enable Ray to keep his commitments without running from one place to another willy-nilly. He arranged for payment of a fee in cases where it was appropriate to do so. He also began calling the people who had big schemes to find out which ones were serious and which were not. With Brotman's help, Ray no longer found himself expected in two or three places at the same time, or needlessly excited by possible deals that had no sound basis. His life was much less confused, but his mind still was. What should he do?

In the end, the choice was taken away from Sugar Ray Leonard. Events over which he had no control made the decision for him.

Cicero Leonard had become ill in Montreal. At the time, everyone thought he was just tired from the trip and all the excitement. But he continued not to feel well. When his condition was diagnosed as meningitis, he was hospitalized. Almost at the same time, Getha Leonard suffered a heart attack. Suddenly, the Leonards were in the deepest financial trouble they had ever known. Sugar Ray understood that he could no longer sit around worrying about what to do. Of the Leonard children, he was the only one in a potential position to make enough money to support his parents and younger sisters, not to mention Juanita and Ray, Jr. And the only way he could hope to realize that potential earning power was to turn pro.

So it was decided: Sugar Ray Leonard was going to turn pro. But he needed to do more than just make that decision to become a professional fighter. He had to have people to represent him in lining up fights, people doing promotional work, people with a legal background who were good at finances, people who knew the game of professional boxing. He also needed money—money to pay all of those people, money for gym use, for equipment, for travel expenses, for the various fees a boxer has to pay the boxing organizations in order to be certified as a professional. When you turn professional, you don't just announce yourself and start fighting. You need a team and you need capital. Sugar Ray didn't have the slightest idea how to get either.

Janks Morton had some ideas. As soon as Ray told him he wanted to turn pro, Morton took him to see Mike Trainer. An attorney in Silver Springs, Maryland, who years before had played on the softball team with Morton, Trainer is white. Ray felt uncomfortable with him at first, even though Morton assured him that Trainer could be trusted completely. It would be months before Sugar Ray and Trainer talked about anything but business, but Trainer was willing to work without a fee, and Sugar Ray needed an unpaid attorney. He certainly did not have the money to pay one!

Trainer did not know a thing about professional boxing, but he was willing to learn. He knew enough about life to know that raising money was the first priority. There were plenty of people who were eager to finance Sugar Ray Leonard's pro career, but Ray did not want to be beholden to any one backer. He didn't want to be owned. It had bothered him to hear professional fight managers talk about "my fighter" or "my boy" long before Muhammad Ali had cautioned him not to sign his life away. So Trainer decided to get a whole group of backers to finance Sugar Ray's career. In this way, he reasoned, no one man would have undue influence.

As soon as word got out, Trainer was besieged by so many calls that he decided to hold a public meeting. At the meeting, he and Sugar Ray learned that many of these people wanted Ray to do more than just box in return for their investment. A store manager wanted him to spend one day a week in his store. A traveling jewelry salesman wanted Ray to go out on the road with him twice a week. Ray could hardly keep up with his other personal appearances, stay in training as a fighter, and do all that, too. Trainer adjourned the meeting.

Puzzling over how to get money for Ray without signing away the young boxer's life, it occurred to Trainer that perhaps the best thing to do would be to take out a loan. That is how he had financed his own law-school education. But the bank officers he approached with the idea didn't think much of it. An educational loan was one thing; a loan to a boxer was quite another. So Trainer decided to go to his own friends and clients. He rounded up 24 people, each of whom agreed to loan Ray $1,000 or less for four years at 8 percent interest. Among them, they put up $21,000, with the promise of nothing in return but their original investment plus interest, *if* Ray succeeded as a professional. No one would have a "piece" of Ray Leonard, a percentage of his earnings, or any hold on him whatsoever once their money was repaid. Sugar Ray Leonard would remain his own man. To make that position even stronger Trainer had papers drawn up creating a corporation called Sugar Ray Leonard, Inc., with Ray himself as the only stockholder. He then signed Ray to a personal services contract with the corporation, at a salary of $475 a week.

Trainer had so little idea of Sugar Ray's potential to earn money as a pro fighter that he had practically picked the sum of $20,000 or so out of a hat. He didn't know if that was enough of a stake to launch the career of a professional fighter. And he certainly didn't know if Ray would earn enough in four years' time to pay back the investors. He told Ray that he might have to take a part-time job at some point, because the investors were his friends and ought to be paid back if at all possible. Still, for the time being they had some money. The next step was to start building an organization.

Naturally, Sugar Ray wanted Dave Jacobs and Janks Morton to be part of that organization, and Mike Trainer was willing to stay on and handle business and legal matters at an hourly fee. None of these people knew much about the world of professional boxing, and they all agreed that they needed someone who knew that world inside out. Charles Brotman was still helping Ray with his scheduling, and he was now asked to find a knowledgeable manager for Sugar Ray. Charles Brotman knew nothing about professional boxing, but he did know the people to call. Before long, even Muhammad Ali's advice had been solicited. Ali's immediate response was: Angelo Dundee.

Angelo Dundee was famous in the boxing world because he had been the trainer of Muhammad Ali since Ali was Cassius Clay. In boxing since 1948, he had learned the game from the gym level up, training fighters of every weight class and level of talent. Dundee was educated to the tricks of the trade by some of the cleverest managers in the history of the game. Although he'd had plenty of experience in the smoke-filled rooms where not-quite-legal deals were made, he had a reputation as a straight shooter. And in a world where making enemies was a fact of life, there was hardly a man who didn't like Dundee. His motto has always been, "It costs nothing to be nice."

Trainer, Brotman, Jacobs, Morton, and Ray himself talked to other managers/trainers, including Eddie Futch and Gil Clancy, but in the end Dundee was chosen. Most of the others wanted Ray to relocate to a city where there was a bigger market and more media, a place like New York or Philadelphia. For Ray, such a move was out of the question. He was a "home boy." He didn't like being away from his family for more than a few days at a time. Angelo Dundee did not ask him to move anywhere. Ray could relate to Dundee's personal style, to his motto about it not costing anything to be

60

nice, and to the fact that Dundee had managed his hero, Muhammad Ali. Besides, Ray decided that Dundee's wife, Helen, reminded him of his mother!

There was no question that Dundee knew boxing. More important, he had connections and the experience to line up the right opponents for Sugar Ray. He knew just about everyone personally, and he could find out quickly about anyone else. He was as comfortable in Latin American boxing circles as in North American ones, for he had trained Cuban fighters before the Castro-led revolution in that country. He spoke fluent Spanish. On top of all this, he was willing to go along with Ray's wish to be his own man. Instead of insisting on 30 percent or more of the money Sugar Ray earned, and on a contract that would effectively bind Ray to him, Dundee agreed to take just 15 percent of Ray's earnings. He would not, however, spend as much time training Sugar Ray as the ordinary manager would. Rather, he would leave most of the training to Dave Jacobs and Janks Morton. Dundee's job would be to select opponents, help promote the fights, and oversee arrangements. He would supervise the last several days of training before a fight, and then take over in Ray's corner during the actual fight.

With the team complete, it was time to plan for Sugar Ray Leonard's debut as a professional boxer. Dundee wanted an opponent who would be a challenge to Ray, but not too big a challenge. It would not do to have Ray lose his first professional fight. On the other hand, it would not do for him to fight a "stiff," a talentless fighter whom he could beat too easily. Dundee wanted the first fight to show that Leonard could carry the potential he'd had as an amateur into the pro game. Plenty of talented amateurs had failed to make this transition.

Eddie Hrica, the "matchmaker" Dundee contacted, offered him a choice of four possible opponents, and from among them Dundee chose Luis (The Bull) Vega, a stocky young fighter from Reading, Pennsylvania, whose record was 14 wins, 8 losses, and 3 knockouts. Vega was tough and had never been knocked off his feet. In Dundee's opinion, if Ray had what it takes to be a pro, he would beat him.

4

THE DRIVE TO THE CHAMPIONSHIP

As soon as Sugar Ray Leonard had announced his intention to turn pro, officials of the city of Baltimore said they would like the city to stage his first pro fight. The commissioner of the city's Civic Center pledged money toward the purse, and CBS-TV matched that sum. Sugar Ray had recently signed on as a boxing analyst with the network, and in January 1977 he worked at ringside when his Olympic teammates Howard Davis and Leon Spinks made their professional debuts. CBS would also broadcast Sugar Ray's first fight in February.

Ray went into prefight training—running, sparring, studying videotapes of Vega's fights. But he spent as much time promoting the fight as he did training for it. In fact, everyone connected with Leonard worked night and day to publicize his first pro match. The reason was that in the fight game today, as in any other sport, you must be "marketable." You must attract a lot of attention and a big audience if you want to have a large purse for your fight and good media coverage. If a lot of people do attend your fight, or watch it on TV, then you can point to those audience figures when negotiating for your next fight.

So the fight was advertised on billboards, posters, and even the backs of buses. The press and the public were invited to watch Leonard work out, and press releases were sent to all the out-of-town newspapers and radio and TV stations. Sugar Ray even sent a telegram to President Jimmy Carter, asking him to attend the fight. It read:

I RESPECTFULLY INVITE YOU AND YOUR FAMILY
TO BE PRESENT AT MY PROFESSIONAL DEBUT IN
BALTIMORE, SATURDAY, FEB. 5 AT 4:30 P.M.
THIS WILL BE MY FIRST BOUT SINCE WINNING
THE OLYMPIC GOLD MEDAL AT MONTREAL. IF
YOU ARE UNABLE TO ATTEND,
PLEASE TUNE IN CBS TELEVISION.
WITH GREAT EXPECTATIONS,
SINCERELY,
SUGAR RAY LEONARD.

On the day before the fight, Sugar Ray took Ray, Jr., to see the movie *Rocky*. The next afternoon, the movie still fresh in his mind, Sugar Ray entered the ring at Baltimore's Civic Center wearing a purple robe he had designed himself. The crowd in the arena numbered 10,270—more than had ever come to a fight there before, even an Ali exhibition fight. They went wild when Leonard arrived, and he smiled, feeling confident. A scowling Luis Vega, looking as tough as his reputation, reminded Leonard that this was no movie. This was the real thing.

The fight began slowly. Sugar Ray danced around

Vega, letting loose quick jabs. Vega stood in the center of the ring, turning to follow the dancing, circling Leonard. When the bell sounded to end the round, Dundee told Leonard to sharpen up, use some combinations, and go in for the attack. Midway through the second round that is just what Leonard began to do. He stopped dancing and went after Vega, banging away at him with furious left-right combinations. He was racking up points on the judges' scorecards. In the fourth round he let loose a string of vicious punches to Vega's face, causing his nose to bleed and gashing the corner of his left eye. The pace slowed in the fifth round, but in the sixth round Leonard was again on the attack. All Vega could do was try to defend himself. When the final bell sounded, there was no question in anyone's mind that the fight was Sugar Ray's. But Vega was still standing, his reputation for never having been knocked off his feet intact. He had indeed been a worthy opponent. Sugar Ray couldn't help thinking that the fight had been almost like a replay of *Rocky*. Vega, he knew, was in his own way a champion.

Sugar Ray was the winner, by unanimous vote of all three judges, who had scored each round, giving points to each fighter. Leonard's professional career had been launched in the best possible way. He had fought well in a well-fought fight, he had won, and with the money he had earned he would be able to pay off his 24 creditors and be beholden to no one. As he put it, he was a free man.

In April, Sugar Ray fought his second pro bout, also in Baltimore, this time against Willie Rodriguez. He won this fight by a decision, too. A large audience watched the match, live and on television. He signed a

After the big win against Vega.

contract with ABC-TV under which the network would broadcast his fights on its "Wide World of Sports," guaranteeing him not just money but a national audience.

His third fight, on June 10, 1977, took place in Hartford, Connecticut. It was staged by an unknown promoter named Dan Doyle, who was head coach of the basketball team at Trinity College in Hartford. Mike Trainer preferred unknown promoters, and Doyle was about as unknown as they come. In fact, Doyle only got into fight promotion because he was writing a graduate-school paper on sports promotion. Doyle guaranteed Sugar Ray $12,000. He made that and more when he beat Vinnie De Barros by a technical knockout (or TKO, when the referee stops the fight because one man is hurt and could be seriously injured if the fight were to continue).

Doyle later staged Leonard fights in Springfield, Massachusetts, and Portland, Maine. Each time the bouts drew record crowds. The fight in Portland drew more people than the Muhammad Ali–Sonny Liston heavyweight title fight in Lewiston, Maine, in 1965. Everything was going according to plan. Trainer knew that if Sugar Ray could draw record crowds in small cities, bigger cities would become interested in staging Leonard fights, too.

Things were also going according to Angelo Dundee's plan. He continued to select opponents who could not beat Leonard, but who were strong and varied in their boxing styles. Each new opponent was just a little bit tougher, making Sugar Ray stretch his skills each time he entered the ring. It was a slow and deliberate way to develop a fighter, but in Dundee's opinion it was the best way. It was paying off.

As 1977 wore on, Sugar Ray piled up more—and more impressive—victories. While his victories over Vega and Rodriguez had been by decision, he'd beaten De Barros with a technical knockout, and he flattened his next three opponents. By February 1978, when he had been boxing professionally just a year, he was meeting opponents for longer scheduled fights, ten rounds instead of six, and developing as a fighter so quickly that Dundee started to feel that the one-step-at-a-time teaching method was too slow.

Sugar Ray met Javier Muniz in New Haven, Connecticut, on March 3, 1978. Muniz had stayed on his feet throughout a ten-round bout against Roberto Duran, a Panamanian known as one of the toughest and most hard-punching welterweights around. Now that Sugar Ray was advancing from six-round to ten-round fights, Dundee wanted an opponent with staying power, and Muniz certainly had gone the distance against Duran. It took Sugar Ray Leonard exactly 2 minutes and 45 seconds to knock him out.

Ray was the only one who was not surprised at the quick knockout. He had studied films of Muniz's earlier fights and identified his weaknesses. In the ring he went to work on them. He did not approach the fight game as a test of strength, but as a test of talent. He relied on cleverness, not brawn. He was as much a student of boxing as he was a practitioner, and he liked nothing better than to spend an evening with his videotape machine and a pile of cassettes of different fights. His approach to his career was exactly that of Trainer and Dundee: Through a well-thought-out plan, they were slowly and deliberately working to make him the welterweight champion, and he was doing everything to reach that goal.

Many fighters can be difficult for their managers and trainers to handle. They slack off on their training, over-eat between fights, party too much, overspend and get into financial trouble. Their trainers and managers must constantly act as parents or baby-sitters, stern authority figures. Sugar Ray Leonard was not one of these fighters. He stayed in shape, mostly by running. Whether a fight was upcoming or not, he made sure he got his rest. He did not party too much, allowed himself to gain only a few pounds over the 147-pound welterweight limit between bouts, and followed the advice of his financial counselors. It had been his decision to turn professional, and he did not expect anyone else but himself to be responsible for him. It was hard to keep on such a straight and narrow path sometimes, but he never allowed himself to lose sight of where that path was going to lead. He was Sugar Ray Leonard and he was going to be the champion.

On he strove toward that goal, winning fight after fight against well-chosen opponents. His other victories in 1978 were against Rocky Ramon (decision), Art Mc Knight (TKO), Bobby Hayman (TKO), Randy Milton (TKO), Rafael Rodriguez (decision), Dick Eklund (decision), Floyd Mayweather (TKO), Randy Shields, who had beaten him in the national AAU finals in 1974 (decision), Bernardo Prada (decision), and Armando Muniz (TKO). All of these bouts were staged in small cities. They were energetically promoted and consistently attracted record audiences. The fight against Armando Muniz in Springfield, Massachusetts, was the last on the contract with ABC-TV. Impressed by its "Wide World of Sports" ratings on the days the Leonard fights were televised, the network contracted with Sugar Ray Leonard, Inc., to televise another five fights.

By March 1979, when he had been fighting professionally just a little over two years, Sugar Ray Leonard was fighting world-ranked boxers, although that distinction was not as awe inspiring as it sounds. Daniel Gonzalez of Argentina was ranked number four in the world but most of his victories had been against unknown boxers in South American villages. Still, the fact that he had world ranking was helpful in promoting the fight, which was held on March 24 in Tucson, Arizona. Sugar Ray had prepared for this fight the same way he had gotten ready for all the others, by training strenuously but also devoting a great deal of time to studying films of Gonzalez's previous fights. As it turned out, he needn't have bothered.

When you are a star, or even well known, in any field you attract people who are known variously as "groupies," "hangers-on," or "leeches." They have many reasons for hanging around. Some want money. Some feel a sense of importance by associating with someone who *is* important. Some, but not many, are real friends. The trouble is that these groupies can become burdens and affect the style of the well-known person. It's said that Elvis Presley and Muhammad Ali were affected by hangers-on. Latin American men, especially, surround themselves with admirers. Sugar Ray Leonard is by nature a loner, and one thing he had decided when he turned pro was to choose a few people he trusted, and to discourage all groupies. Daniel Gonzalez had allowed a great many people to attach themselves to him.

How the presence or absence of a bunch of followers can affect a fighter was shown that afternoon in Tucson.

Before the fight, in a room off a narrow corridor of the arena at the Tucson Community Center, Sugar Ray Leonard warmed up under the watchful eyes of Janks Morton, Dave Jacobs, and Angelo Dundee. Except for brief visits from his mother and Juanita, no other people were allowed near Sugar Ray. Ray had decided to try a new brand of gloves. These gloves were more uniformly padded and made more impact than his old gloves, which had more padding around the knuckles. After checking to make sure Ray's gloves were comfortable, Dundee sauntered out to the corridor and to the room next door, where Gonzalez was.

The room was so full of people that Dundee couldn't see Gonzalez. Men sat on chairs and tables, or leaned against the walls. Dundee's first thought was that with all these people in the room, Gonzalez could not warm up properly. And when he finally spied the fighter, he knew he was right. Gonzalez wasn't even sweating. Dundee didn't have to hang around any longer. He went back to Leonard's room and told Sugar Ray to "nail" Gonzalez at the first opportunity.

Sugar Ray did just that. In the first round he knocked Gonzalez down with a quick left-right combination. Although Gonzalez got up immediately, he was none too steady. His eyes were glassy and he spit out his mouthpiece. Then Leonard finished him off with a right-left-right combination. After exactly two minutes and three seconds the fight was over.

The cheers for the victorious Leonard were mixed with boos. The crowd hadn't gotten its money's worth! Even Sugar Ray's mother had a complaint. As usual, she had taken a tranquilizer, but there wasn't enough time for it to take effect and wear off. How could she celebrate her son's victory tranquilized? Sugar Ray had exerted himself so little that he did not even need a shower.

His next fight, against Adolfo Viruet in Las Vegas in April, was not so easy. It went the full ten rounds and Sugar Ray won by a decision. The following match was even tougher, teaching him a lesson he would not soon forget.

Sugar Ray was not used to being hit solidly. He had the ability to move around so that most of his opponents' punches glanced off him. The few times he had taken a solid punch, the blow had been to his body, not to his head. But in this fight, staged in Baton Rouge, Louisiana, on May 20, 1979, Marcos Geraldo hit him square in the head with such impact that he reeled. Dizzied, he tried to focus on his opponent, but could not. He danced back and forth, trying to make three Geraldos blend into one, but they wouldn't. Sugar Ray didn't know which of the three targets he saw was the real one. He backed off, hoping that more distance would sharpen his vision. The three Geraldos came after him, and one of them hit him again. Amazingly, the second punch cleared his head. The two shadow Geraldos merged into the middle one. But even with just one target in front of him, Sugar Ray was in trouble. He'd been hit hard. To regain his strength and his timing, he needed more than a few brief moments in his corner between rounds. He had to recover in the ring —recover and emerge victorious.

He would later say that he learned survival in that fight. He had to reach down deep inside himself, and bring up every ounce of strength and will. He had to dance and feint as he never had before to buy time, to regain his rhythm. He did it, and he won the fight by decision. He also won considerable respect in boxing circles. More than a few observers had criticized him as a phoney fighter created largely by the media and clever advisers. They said he was a fighter who'd had it too easy, who hadn't really been tested, who'd been coddled and brought along inch by inch, who wouldn't show any stamina when the chips were down. Against Marcos Geraldo he had shown that he had more than just speed and a bunch of pretty combination punches. He also had strength and, most important of all, will. He had shown himself a worthy contender for the welter-weight championship of the world.

The stage was now set for Sugar Ray to challenge Wilfredo Benitez, World Boxing Council welterweight champion. Leonard's advisers contacted Benitez's manager, Jimmy Jacobs. He was eager to talk about a title fight. There was a lot of negotiating. Both Mike Trainer, who did the negotiating for Sugar Ray, and Jimmy Jacobs wanted his fighter to get the biggest share of the money the bout would bring. Jacobs insisted that Benitez, a Puerto Rican, deserved the bigger share because he was the champion. Trainer pointed out that Benitez had never earned more than $150,000 for a fight. Sugar Ray Leonard was already earning more than that. It was Leonard who would attract the audiences, and the big money from television. There were negotiations with the three major television networks and with possible promoters.

Bob Arum, who with Don King reigns as the king of the really big fight promotions, was chosen by Trainer and Jacobs. The championship bout between Wilfredo Benitez and Sugar Ray Leonard soon became one of the richest in the history of boxing. Leonard, by virtue of his drawing power, and Benitez, because he was the champion, would each make at least a million dollars from the fight. This was a first in welterweight history. The fight date was set for November 30, 1979, in Las Vegas.

Meanwhile, Sugar Ray Leonard kept boxing. He beat Tony Chiaverini, a left-hander out of Kansas City, by a TKO. He beat Pete Ranzany, the North American Boxing Federation welterweight champion, the same way, but this time he did it in front of his "nicknamesake," Sugar Ray Robinson. Not only did Robinson attend the fight, and Leonard thought that was honor enough, but he also took steps to squelch any resentment other people felt about Leonard's use of his nickname. Some people in boxing circles called Leonard arrogant for using the name of a fighter as great as Robinson, but Robinson said he was gratified by it. In his opinion, it showed how much Leonard thought of him. It was a compliment. And the way Sugar Ray fought that night was a compliment to the boxing tradition.

On September 28, 1979, Sugar Ray polished off Andy Price, a tough Californian who was supposed to have given him trouble, with eight seconds left in the first round. But this last victory did not please Angelo Dundee. He'd planned the Price match as a warm-up for the Benitez fight, for Price's style of fighting was similar to that of Benitez. Now, Sugar Ray would have to train very carefully if he expected to beat Benitez, who was undefeated.

Benitez was enjoying his third championship, having

won the junior middleweight and junior welterweight titles before claiming the welterweight crown. Benitez was far more experienced in the pro game than Leonard. Although he was two years younger than Sugar Ray, he had been fighting longer. He was only 17 when he won his first world title, and by the time he was 18 he had two titles. He was a clever fighter, as good with his left hand as he was with his right. Benitez was a counterpuncher, and some people said he was the best defensive boxer in the game. He was also accustomed to going 15 rounds. Sugar Ray Leonard had never gone more than 10.

On top of all this, Sugar Ray went into his bout against Benitez with a slight cramp in his natural style, thanks to some well-meant advice from his idol and sometime-mentor Muhammad Ali. Ali called him the night before the match and cautioned him not to try to do anything cute or flashy. The judges, Ali said, would resent it if Sugar Ray tried to do any hotdogging against a world champion. Sugar Ray took Ali's advice.

Six months earlier, Sugar Ray Leonard would probably have taken Ali's advice, but he also might have resented it. Six months earlier he was so busy pursuing his goal of being champion that he resented many things that seemed to get in his way. But as plans for his challenge fight against Benitez had been set and training had got underway, his chance to reach the goal he'd kept uppermost in his mind for two and a half years approached. He began to look at a lot of things differently. He felt his mind calming down. As he put it, he started feeling "settle-minded." He began to look at his whole life—not just the future, but also the past and the present. He realized he was nearing a major crossroads in his life, and he also realized that whichever road he took, that road had to lead somewhere. It was time to pay some attention to his life outside the ring, and to get that life in order, and that meant setting a date to marry Juanita.

He shared his feelings with his fiancée not long before the fight. He expected that she would want to set the earliest date possible, but he was wrong. Though Juanita was overjoyed that the man she loved and the father of her child had finally decided to marry her, she had her own ideas about how things should proceed. She wanted a June wedding, she solemnly told her long-time husband-to-be. Laughing happily, he agreed. They announced the date just before Sugar Ray entered the ring at Caesar's Palace, just before the biggest fight of his career. Win or lose, Sugar Ray Leonard would marry his childhood sweetheart, Juanita Wilkinson, on June 28, 1980.

On the night of November 30, 1979, Sugar Ray Leonard and Wilfredo Benitez faced off in a fight that was the biggest match of both careers. For a full 30 seconds at the beginning of round one, they stared at each other, their faces just inches apart, each trying to psych the other. But for both of them, it was like looking into a mirror. Each saw in the other's face the same determination.

Sugar Ray made the first move. Jabbing with his left, working his left jab–right jab–left hook combination, he scored quickly against his opponent in the first round and again in the third round, when he knocked Benitez to the floor with a left jab. Through the third round, it looked as if Sugar Ray Leonard had the fight under control, but when the bell rang to start round four the situation changed remarkably. It was as if a new Wilfredo Benitez came out of the opposite corner.

Not only did he duck or otherwise evade most of Sugar Ray's punches, he started landing some of his own. He scored twice with his right in the fourth round, all the while rendering Leonard's right overhand practically useless with his defensive tactics. Angelo Dundee finally told Leonard to forget that particular punch and "go downstairs," or concentrate on body punches.

For those in the audience it was a rare display of ringcraft. Neither man was able to control the fight. Sugar Ray Leonard was amazed at how his opponent evaded his punches. No one had ever caused him to miss so many. The part of him that was able to detach itself from the fight, that could figuratively stand back and watch what was going on, couldn't help marveling at how good Benitez was. No doubt that same part of Benitez was saying the same thing about Sugar Ray. Maybe these parts of both fighters were doing that when they actually cracked their foreheads together in the sixth round. Benitez got the worst of it. The collision resulted in a gash in his forehead, a wound that could be reopened with a well-placed punch from Leonard. Sugar Ray got only a welt on his forehead.

On they fought. Benitez was hampered by the forehead wound and by a sore left thumb, which he had hurt earlier in the fight. He still cleverly avoided most of Leonard's punches. In the ninth round, Sugar Ray scored with a combination that put Benitez up against the ropes. In the eleventh he delivered a hook with such force that it jarred loose his opponent's mouthpiece. But Benitez got in some scoring punches, too. As the bell ended the fourteenth round, neither fighter, nor the men in their corners, could be at all certain how the three judges' scorecards looked. The fight had been so close that both believed they needed to win the fifteenth round. They came out with a flurry of punches in that last round, trying everything they knew, reaching into their bags of punches to come up with something that would catch the other off guard. Sugar Ray decided to try a punch he had been studying—a left uppercut that bantamweight champion Wilfredo Gomez used to perfection. He'd been watching films of Gomez fights for weeks. Since his overhand right hadn't worked, he decided to try a punch that was almost the exact opposite. He stepped inside and delivered it, and Benitez went down on his knees. Though Benitez was up quickly, he was clearly dazed. Leonard used the advantage, throwing two more punches. Referee Carlos Padilla stopped the fight with six seconds to go.

It took Sugar Ray Leonard a couple of seconds to realize what had happened. Then it dawned on him— he was the welterweight champion of the world! He had reached the milestone he and Trainer and Dundee and Jacobs and Morton had been aiming for since he'd decided to turn pro. He was the champ, and he had just finished the longest and most well-fought bout of his young career. It was a proud night for Sugar Ray. In fact, it was a proud night for boxing. The two men had displayed the sport at its best, and afterward they displayed sportsmanship at its best. At the press conference following the fight, even the loser seemed happy. Although the $1.2 million he would collect probably had something to do with his attitude, Benitez seemed genuinely pleased for the man who had just taken away his title. Sugar Ray was a great fighter, he told the assembled reporters. Wilfredo Benitez was a great fighter, Sugar Ray insisted. The two men embraced several times. As it turned out, Sugar Ray would have won by decision even without the TKO ruling by referee Carlos Padilla, although by only 2 points out of a possible 136. Even if the two opponents had been tied on the judges' scorecards, there were not many who would have criticized Padilla's decision to end the fight when he did. For as Leonard and Benitez went at each other, a middleweight boxer named Willie Classen lay unconscious in a New York City hospital, suffering from a brutal beating in the ring. He would die a few days later, and the realization that boxing could be a fatal game was very much on the minds of everyone in boxing at that time.

Although his life had never been in danger during the match, Sugar Ray Leonard was feeling the brutality of the game himself. He did not attend any of the postfight celebrations of his victory. He had sweat so much that his body was suffering from water loss, or dehydration. He was as sore as he had ever been in his life. Every bone in his body ached, and, what was even worse in his opinion, his face was bruised. In addition to the welt on his forehead, he had bruises under his eyes. He didn't like that one bit. Still, in a way he felt that the bruises were like badges of courage. He had faced the most important test of his career so far—and prevailed.

At the age of 23, Sugar Ray Leonard was welterweight champion of the world—at least of the WBC world, for the WBA recognized its own champions. His possibilities were almost limitless. Not only did he hold the title, but he was credited with almost single-handedly elevating the welterweight class to an importance approaching the heavyweight class of boxing. No other welterweight had ever attracted such large live audiences, or so much attention from television, or so many product-endorsement offers, or so much money for fights. He was now in a position to choose whoever he wanted to fight, to have the major say in where and when he fought, and to command bigger and bigger fight purses.

He was also in a position to retire. He had done what he set out to do, which was to become the champion and make a lot of money. Juanita reminded him of that. So did his mother. His advisers also remembered what he had said about wanting to stay in professional boxing only until he reached certain stated goals. They were prepared to advise him how best to end his career. But Sugar Ray Leonard, having reached a point where he could retire if he wanted to, decided not to retire after all. He enjoyed being the champion, and he wanted a chance to defend his title. He wanted to show that winning it was not a fluke, that he was not just the champion but the best welterweight in the world. And he still had the desire, voiced when he turned pro, to do something really big, something special.

There were people in boxing who resented the fact that Sugar Ray was the WBC champion. They didn't believe he had "paid his dues." He hadn't been in the business long enough or fought against opponents who were tough enough. He had been coddled by his advisers. He had been given too much money and too much media exposure in exchange for too little work. A lot of this criticism stemmed from jealousy, and jealousy has a way of causing people to overlook things like Leonard's performances against Geraldo and even Benitez. Sugar Ray realized this, but he didn't like hearing people say that there were lots of welterweights around who could cream him if they had a chance to meet him in the ring. He wanted to prove them wrong. Besides, he would be a fool not to make a few more millions while he had the chance. So, he told his advisers to start considering the requests from prospective title challengers and he told Juanita and the rest of his family that he wasn't ready to retire.

Juanita and his mother were not happy about his decision, but there was not much they could do about it. Sugar Ray Leonard's mind was made up. It was important to him, and in his opinion it was important to their future security, that he remain in the pro game and defend his title.

By now, everyone close to Sugar Ray Leonard had benefited so much from his pro fighting career that they found it hard to argue with him. Just as he had set out to do, he had become the major, if not the sole, provider for them. He had been generous with his fight earnings. His parents had a new house in a nice section of Palmer Park; they also had a hefty bank account. His brothers and sisters had new cars and money for college, if they wanted to go. He and Juanita had their own apartment, and Little Ray had all the clothes he needed, all the toys he could play with. The people who had stood by him in the early days had not been forgotten. Dave Jacobs, for example, now had a new house, two cars, and his own sizable bank account. None of these people felt so beholden to Ray that they couldn't advise him to quit pro boxing, but all of them owed him enough to allow him to make his own decisions.

Childhood sweethearts, married in Landover, Maryland.

Juanita Wilkinson was the only exception. She had carried a special burden, one not so easily repaid, and perhaps this had something to do with her decision not to put off their wedding until June. Ray was champion now, on top of the world, and Juanita did not want to be left out. She did not like the limelight. She wouldn't go around wearing lots of expensive jewelry or furs just because Ray was making big money, but she did feel it was time for her to be married to Ray in the eyes of the law, as well as in the eyes of other women. She tried not to feel insecure, but it had been hard, as Ray had become richer and more famous, for her to see the way other women looked at him and not worry that he might decide he was tired of her. She had deliberately not made many friends among women her own age, for fear that they might use her to get to Ray, but she realized she would not be able to control whom he met now that he was the champion. Although she had always dreamed of a June wedding, Juanita had learned that one is usually better off thinking realistically.

The wedding was held early, on January 19, 1980. Six-year-old Ray, Jr., was the ring bearer. They had a brief vacation in California and Las Vegas, and planned a real honeymoon trip for when Ray had more time. At that point, he did not have the time. As the champion he was expected to defend his title at least three times in 1980. Already his first bout had been scheduled for March 31, two months away. Juanita understood that her new husband could not take time for a honeymoon right then. She told Ray that when they could take time for a honeymoon, she wanted him to be in one piece. To her mind the odds were against his staying that way if he spent much more time in the ring.

Ironically, it was not Sugar Ray but the first challenger for his title who really risked staying whole in the next fight. Britain's Davey "Boy" Green was the first welterweight to get a chance at the big money and the media exposure that a bout against Sugar Ray Leonard now guaranteed. In the fourth round of a not particularly exciting fight in Landover, Maryland, Sugar Ray, who had publicly vowed never again to cramp his own style, knocked out Green with a punch so hard that Green lay on the canvas without moving for several minutes.

It was long enough for Sugar Ray Leonard to confront the other side of the two-sided coin of boxing. One side of this coin is boxing at its best—an intricate game, even a beautiful game, when two opponents confront each other in a test not just of will but also of technique, when defense is as important as offense (although audiences still think of boxing as a totally offensive game). On this side of the coin, no one gets seriously hurt, because both opponents are so clever on defense that they are able to evade savage blows. The other side of the coin is boxing at its worst—improperly matched players. Perhaps one is the "fall guy," whether predetermined or not; or two well-matched players, one of whom gets caught off guard and is defenseless, with a referee who does nothing to stop the fight. Perhaps the attacker forgets that it is all a game and moves in for the kill; or the attacker realizes exactly what has happened and gets the sinking feeling that in the course of a game he has done something that isn't play at all but a matter of life and death. In the last case, there is no one to blame but the sport itself.

Everyone who knows boxing knows that serious injuries, even death, can result when two men enter a ring intent on knocking each other out. Most of the time, a boxer worries about getting hurt himself, but there are occasions when he is reminded that he is just as capable of doing harm. The two hands he has trained to put points on judges' scorecards are also capable of inflicting permanent damage to human beings. Boxing is neither game nor sport when one boxer permanently injures or kills another. When Davey "Boy" Green fell to the canvas and did not move, Sugar Ray Leonard felt a cold, creeping fear spread over his entire body, numbing it, chilling his brain except for one terrible thought: What if he doesn't get up? And when at last Green did stir and finally got up and walked unsteadily out of the ring to his locker room, the cold, numb feeling did not leave Sugar Ray. He went through the motions of raising his arms and acknowledging his victory, but his mind was still on that question: What if?

For days afterward, he couldn't stop thinking about how Green had looked lying motionless on the floor of the ring and how he himself had felt during those interminably long minutes. He, who was so worried about even getting his face bruised, had delivered a punch so hard that it had knocked a man unconscious. What would have happened if Green had been killed or suffered some permanent injury? Would the money and the media exposure—would anything—have been worth the price of a man's life or health? Did he really want to go on in this game that could be fatal? It was a wiser Ray Leonard who decided to continue, with the knowledge that he wasn't just putting his own life on the line when he went into the ring. He was facing an opponent whose life he might also control.

5
SUGAR RAY MEETS ROBERTO DURAN

By the time Sugar Ray Leonard had beaten Davey "Boy" Green, a lot of people in boxing were saying that he was overdue for a real challenge. None of his earlier opponents had been of his caliber (which was strange sounding to those who considered Wilfredo Benitez a true champion). How about Pipino Cuevas, these critics suggested?

Cuevas, a Mexican fighter, was the welterweight champion of the WBA. Leonard's critics charged that he'd chosen to fight Benitez, the WBC champion, because he was afraid to fight Cuevas. Cuevas was a good match for Leonard not just because of his prowess as a boxer but because he was champion of the welterweight division of the rival boxing organization. A match between Cuevas and Leonard would pit the WBA and WBC titleholders against one another. The match would decide, at least on paper, who really had the right to be called "World" Champion in the welterweight division. Boxing people called this "unifying the title."

But politics soon came into play, as so often happens

in boxing. There were people who didn't want Leonard to fight Cuevas. They wanted him to fight Roberto Duran.

Duran was a Panamanian fighter who had made his career, his fame, and whatever money had come his way as a lightweight. He had recently moved up to the welterweight class. Although Duran was a hero in his native Panama and quite a celebrity in other parts of Latin America, he had not made much money from his 70-odd pro fights. Now, he and his managers were looking for a big fight, one that would get him the money and the attention they thought he deserved. In their eyes, Sugar Ray Leonard was the key to all this money and attention. In the welterweight class, only a fight with Leonard could bring big television contracts and all the other "gravy" that Duran had never enjoyed. But if Leonard fought Cuevas and lost to him, Duran would never get the chance. The people behind Duran were afraid that Sugar Ray would lose to Cuevas.

Much pressure was put on Cuevas. He was informed by the WBA that he could not meet Leonard in a title bout. Cuevas's advisers said that was all right, they would go for a nontitle bout. But that wouldn't do either. Even if he fought Leonard in a nontitle match, Cuevas was told, he would be stripped of his title by the WBA. In April, plans for a Leonard-Cuevas bout were cancelled without much explanation.

When he heard of the cancellation, Dick Young, a sportswriter for the New York *Daily News,* charged "conspiracy." In his column he exposed the behind-the-scenes pressures that had prevented the Leonard-Cuevas fight while promoting the Leonard-Duran fight. But even Young had a hard time detailing the charges of conspiracy so his readers could understand them. It was all very complicated. Although the WBA, based in Mexico, was supposed to be the rival of the WBC, based in Panama, Panamanians had a great deal of influence in the WBA. The president of the WBA, Rodrigo Sanchez, was a Panamanian by birth, and he was strongly influenced by the Panamanian government. The Panamanian government wanted its countryman, Roberto Duran, to fight Sugar Ray Leonard. It put pressure on Sanchez to see that this was made possible. One of Duran's people insisted that the Panamanian government had only "requested" that the Leonard-Cuevas fight be postponed, but no one in the boxing world thought much of that weak excuse. Still, there wasn't much anyone who objected to all this playing of politics could do. The WBA and the WBC make their own rules, and they are both based in countries where the idea of government regulation has a different meaning than it does in the United States.

Serious boxing fans had no desire to see the Leonard-Cuevas fight reinstated, and they didn't care what the reasons were for the cancellation. A bout between Duran and Leonard could be far more exciting than one between Cuevas and Leonard. It would be a clash of fighting styles as different as night and day. Next to the prospect of such a match, considerations like "unifying the title" just had to take a back seat. Who cared about the on-paper world champion? A Leonard-Duran fight would be real.

It wasn't long before promoters Bob Arum and Don King were talking terms, and their styles of doing business were as different as Duran's and Leonard's styles of fighting. Arum, a lawyer like Mike Trainer, looked as if he went to Wall Street every day. He wore pin-striped suits, visited a barbershop regularly, and approached fight promotion like an accountant, rarely letting his own personality get in the way of business. By contrast, Don King's personality was part of his business. Although he dressed in suits, his hair stood out from his head as if he'd just put his finger in an electrical socket. His hair had become a trademark of sorts, and probably he needed a special barber to keep it looking that way. He had another trademark, a crown, and he made great use of it for the fights he promoted. In those fights there were always advertising poles in the ring with crowns on them, and often a huge crown emblazoned on the center of the canvas. Don King had received his education on the streets. He had served a prison term for manslaughter. But he was no less smart than Arum. He never let his flamboyance get in the way of his money sense. Anyone who dismissed him as all flash and no sense wound up with a lousy deal, or with no deal at all.

The promoters squared off and before long they had a deal that would break all previous records for boxing money. The fight was on for June 20, 1980, in Montreal, Canada.

Just about the only thing that Sugar Ray Leonard and Roberto Duran had in common, except that they were both excellent welterweight boxers, was that they had both grown up poor. But "poor" means different things in Panama than it does in the United States. Roberto Duran had known poverty and hardship that Sugar Ray Leonard could barely imagine.

Roberto Duran was born in Chorillo, a poor section of Panama City. Except for a brief time in a country town about 150 miles away, that is where he also grew up. He did not meet his father until he was 21 years old. His father was in the military and traveled around a lot. Just about every time he visited his wife, he left her with another baby, but no financial support. Roberto can remember ten times when his mother was forced to give him away to anyone who would feed him. Roberto was the second oldest of nine children. There was never a time when the family was not hungry, and there was never a time in Roberto's memory when he wasn't grubbing for food. He speared fish, stole fruit, and learned early that in a neighborhood where everyone was poor, he had better know how to fight. If he wasn't fighting hunger, he was fighting other kids. He was expelled for fighting so often that when he finally left school at age 14 he was only in the third grade.

Roberto started out in amateur boxing at the age of ten. He fought exactly 16 amateur fights (and won 13 of them) before turning professional in 1967, at the age of 17. The purse for his first pro fight was $25. By the time anyone cared enough to train and guide him, his boxing style was set. He was a street fighter and nothing could change his basic brawling, mauling style. What those who did train him taught him was to be more scientific about his offense, and how to escape being punched back.

The young man whom friends called "Cholo," which roughly translated means "one whose hair is hard to comb," started out as a lightweight. But if his weight was light, his punches were not. He just bulldozed over his opponents, winning by knockouts in the majority of his fights. It wasn't long before he received a professional nickname, as most fighters do. His was "Manos de Piedra" (Hands of Stone).

Duran did not lose a single fight in his first four years as a professional. At the age of 21 he was beaten in a ten-round fight by Esteban DeJesus, and he did not react well to the loss. He beat the walls of his bathroom until his fists were bloody and vowed to get even with DeJesus. He got the chance to do so twice, in 1974 and 1978, both times by savage knockouts.

By the time Duran beat DeJesus for the second time, he was having serious trouble keeping his weight down to the 135-pound lightweight limit. Roberto liked to eat, and like many people who have grown up poor and hungry he found it impossible to control his urge for food. He would balloon up to 170 pounds when he wasn't in training for a fight, and even when he was in training his manager and trainers would almost literally starve him to ensure that he made weight. They knew that he would always get friends to sneak him a few steaks. By 1978 it was just too hard for him to get down to 135 pounds. After defeating Esteban DeJesus, Duran gave up his lightweight title and joined the welterweight class, where the weight limit was 147 pounds.

He was equally successful as a welterweight, beating all eight of the opponents he faced. By the time his fight against Sugar Ray Leonard was set, he had won 69 professional fights, 55 of them by knockouts, and lost only once. He wasn't going to let a young pipsqueak like Sugar Ray Leonard put a second fight in his loss column. Still, his punches had not been as devastating against the heavier fighters, and he had not been matched against more than a couple of fighters with prowess like his own.

Sugar Ray Leonard knew that Roberto Duran was going to be his toughest opponent yet. He knew about Duran's career and was aware of the excitement the impending match had caused in boxing circles, even before the fight was officially announced. As a sportswriter for the Indianapolis *Star* wrote, it was "the most anticipated nonheavyweight fight since Sugar Ray Robinson fought Randy Turpin and Carmen Basilio in the 1950s." The excitement generated by the Leonard-Duran fight was the kind that sharks must feel when they smell blood. The general feeling was that Sugar Ray Leonard had had it too easy and if anyone could give him his comeuppance it was the slugger and mauler Duran. Knowing all this, it was hard for Ray not to be intimidated. Duran's attitude at the Waldorf Astoria in New York the night the fight was officially announced didn't make him feel any more comfortable.

Of course there's always some showboating on such nights. The boxers, even if they are good friends outside the ring, have to pretend they are out for blood. It is expected of them. They are supposed to try to intimidate their opponents, preferably in clever ways that the sportswriters can report in their columns the next day. Muhammad Ali was a master at that. Colorful reportage by the sportswriters would generate interest in the fight, stimulate ticket sales, attract TV advertisers, and all that. Ray Leonard knew that was as important a part of the fight game as the actual bout. But that night at the Waldorf he knew that Roberto Duran wasn't playing. As the two men faced each other in front of the TV news cameras, Duran held his fist up in Leonard's face. "June twentieth," he said, "June twentieth." There was no question about what his eyes said he planned to do on that date two months away. This wasn't just for the reporters and the cameras and microphones. There was real hatred in Duran's eyes, and Leonard was momentarily taken aback. He recovered quickly. "When I fight Roberto Duran," he announced, "I don't just want to beat him. I want to kill him!" His eyes flashed and he had that look that he got when he entered the ring. Those close to him had never seen that look on his face outside the ring. Later, when reporters asked him why he had not been his usual happy and clever-speaking self, he explained that he was just talking language that Duran would understand, beating him to the punch. In Leonard's opinion, Duran would have said he was going to kill Leonard, if Leonard hadn't said it first. Sugar Ray also assured the reporters that he would not change his style to fight Duran. He intended to beat him to the punch in the ring, too. Of course, what a professional athlete and public personality says and what he thinks are often two different things.

Sugar Ray Leonard was not interested in killing, or being killed. He didn't want to get any scars, or knots from calcium buildup. He didn't consider wounds a necessary part of fighting. He didn't care about staying in boxing a long time. All he wanted to do was establish himself as a champion and make enough money to take good care of his family and friends. Then he would retire. He had regarded the fight against Duran as a business venture in which they both would make a lot of money and he would be established as a top contender. But Duran had turned the coming bout into something more personal, and that both scared and excited Sugar Ray.

Both fighters went immediately into training. Duran and his entourage went to Grossinger's, a resort in New York's Catskill Mountains. He trained harder than he had in years. He knew that some people were whispering that he didn't have the self-discipline to keep his weight down and really get into shape. He knew that some people thought his age would work against him. At 29, he was old for a fighter, and the five years' difference between his age and Leonard's was not a minor factor. He was shorter than Leonard by two and a half inches. His reach was seven inches shorter. He knew that people were taking such statistics into account when they explained why they favored Leonard to win. But Duran was studying films of Leonard's fights, and though he regarded Leonard as a good boxer, Duran was confident that through his skills and sheer determination, he could emerge the victor.

Leonard went to his training camp in New Carrolton, Maryland. He, too, worked out with particular seriousness. He studied films of Duran fights over and over. Watching his future opponent's moves, he tried to find weaknesses and ways that he could use his own best moves to particular advantage. It was clear from the films that Duran usually controlled a fight. He was good at "cutting off the ring," forcing his opponent to stand still and fight. Once he'd cornered his opponent, he had, basically, a nonmoving target for his hammerlike blows.

Although odds makers favored Leonard to win the fight by a 9 to 5 edge, there were many who ques-

Angelo Dundee checks Leonard's weight.

tioned Sugar Ray's ability to withstand Duran's vicious punches, and Leonard knew it. He felt a compulsion to "stand up and take it like a man." For this reason, plus what he saw in Duran's fight films, he disagreed with Angelo Dundee about the best approach to take against the Panamanian. Dundee wanted him to dance around, to feint left and move right, to move from side to side, not to get caught on the ropes. Stay away from Duran, he advised; give yourself enough room to make your left jab really count. But Sugar Ray's mind was made up: He wasn't going to run, he was going to stand and fight. He was going to put as much pressure on Duran as Duran put on him.

As June 20 approached, the odds makers continued to favor Sugar Ray, but even he admitted that Duran was winning what sportswriters called the "Psych Fight." While Duran appeared confident, even cocky, Sugar Ray become more withdrawn and nervous. The fight was to be staged in Montreal, and as the date neared both men arrived in Canada to continue their training. Their respective "handlers" got down to the technical business of rules discussions, choosing the place and time for the official weigh-in, etc. Ray Arcel, Duran's trainer, also started a campaign to make sure the referee didn't interfere too much in the fight.

The referee is a very important man in a boxing match. He decides if a foul has been committed. He breaks apart the two fighters when they are in a clutch. He decides when to start and when to stop counting when a fighter goes down. And he decides if and when to stop a fight before the official number of rounds is over. He also has a say in scoring the match, along with the judges. Some referees are "active," calling many fouls and frequently breaking up clutches. Others are inclined to let the boxers go at each other and to step into the fight only when the most blatant fouls are being committed. Because of Duran's fighting style, his people decided that the latter type of referee would be preferable. In the final days before the fight they took steps to ensure that the referee, Carlos Padilla, would not be too active.

They did this by publicly expressing concern that Padilla would inhibit Duran and not allow him to fight his way. Padilla would call too many fouls and break up Duran's rhythm, they said. Later, Angelo Dundee would charge that by expressing these concerns, Duran's people had inhibited Padilla.

Dundee should know. He had learned many tricks of the trade from the wily old Arcel. Way back in the late 1940s, when Dundee was just starting out in the fight business, he saw a fighter of Arcel's knock his opponent down. As the referee started the count, Arcel climbed into the ring and acted as if he was throwing a robe over his fighter's shoulders. This action distracted the referee and confused him long enough so that he counted the opponent out even though the man had actually gotten up in time. Dundee considered this a clever trick and later used it himself. Unfortunately, he couldn't figure out how to counter Arcel's public statements about Padilla so that Padilla would not feel intimidated.

The final days ticked away. Suddenly, there was a new problem. In the course of a prefight physical that included an electrocardiograph, Duran showed signs of a heart condition. He was given further tests, and the official verdict was that his heart had given off so-called

abnormal patterns because he was a particularly powerful athlete. He had a cold, but that was all.

To help promote interest in the fight, there was an
unofficial weigh-in on Wednesday, June 18. Duran and
Leonard sat on opposite sides of the room. Duran kept
holding up two fingers and shouting at Ray, "Two days
more. Two days more and I am champion."

In response, Sugar Ray smiled and blew a kiss at
Duran. "I love you," he called back. Duran's response
was a string of Spanish unprintables.

Sugar Ray admitted that he was a little afraid of
Duran. The Panamanian's reactions, style, and charac-
ter were like nothing he had ever encountered before.
As he told reporters, "He's so—what do they call it—
ferocious. . . ."

The big night came at last. Montreal's Olympic Stadium was packed with over 45,000 people, ranging
from the beautiful and famous in the $500 ringside seats
to average folks who'd paid $20 for the rafters. They
buzzed with anticipation. They buzzed all through the
preliminary fights, those minor bouts that are always on
a boxing "card." These fights give the audience something more for their money, while giving less well
known fighters some exposure. One of those less well
known fighters was Sugar Ray's older brother Roger,
who had turned pro after getting out of the Air Force.
In the first bout of the night he beat Clyde Gray in a
junior middleweight contest. Happily, he returned to
the dressing room he shared with Ray. His younger
brother congratulated him almost in an offhand way.
Roger asked what was wrong. Sugar Ray would not tell
him. Only later was he able to put into words the way
he suddenly felt. He had felt lost, he explained. All the

momentum, all the excitement just vanished. He had gotten caught up in the "hype," the media attention, the verbal sparring with Duran, all the publicity about Duran's savagery and bad-guy image, all the questions about whether he, Sugar Ray, could take Duran's punches. He had thought he understood the media and could use it for his own benefit. He had believed that he could play "the game" without losing his concentration or taking any of what went on personally. But he had underestimated the power of all that publicity. He later compared the hype to a spider's web and himself to a fly. The fly has no trouble crawling around the web until it hits one of the sticky spots. Once it does, the fly can't get out—the web has caught it.

The time came for the big fight, the title fight, the fight the audience had been waiting for. Duran entered the ring first, blowing kisses at the crowd and raising his arms to his cheering supporters. Then Sugar Ray arrived. As he entered the ring, he couldn't help remembering how he had entered the same ring, in the same stadium, back in 1976. After the Olympics he had wanted to retire from boxing. Now here he was back again, hoping that a win tonight would make it easier for him to retire soon from professional boxing. But, as he later said, there was no adrenaline flowing through his body. He went through the motions of waving at his cheering supporters, but he felt like a robot. Instead of "playing to the crowd," as he could do so well, he simply opened his arms as if to accept the homage due him. Then he turned toward Duran for the traditional prefight tap of gloves. But Duran was having none of that. He refused the tap, and once again Ray Leonard was reminded how little he understood his opponent.

The three judges, from three different countries, signified that they were ready. The referee gave his instructions. The opening bell rang, and the two fighters squared off, jockeying for position. Ray dealt out a lightning-quick left jab that found its target, but that was the one good punch he managed in the entire three minutes. Duran just swarmed over him, driving him toward the ropes with a furious flurry of punches. Always moving forward, he forced Sugar Ray along the ropes from one corner to another, scoring repeatedly with lefts and rights inside. To Leonard and his fans, the three-minute round was like a nightmare in slow motion.

In the second round, Duran again took immediate control, forcing Leonard to the ropes. He caught Ray with a solid left hook followed by an overhand right that pinned him in the corner for most of the round. The referee did little to control the infighting, and when the gong sounded Sugar Ray looked dazed.

By the end of the third round, Juanita was crying in her ringside seat and Ray's younger sister Sharon was trying to comfort her. To most people in the arena it didn't look as if the scheduled 15-round fight could go more than 5 rounds. Sugar Ray just wouldn't be able to hold up under Duran's mauling. But Leonard showed that he was made of stronger stuff. The punch in the second round may have dazed him, but it also woke him up and caused him to "find" himself. By the fourth round he wasn't even trying to dance or move or jab. He stood head to head with Duran, clutching, grabbing, and fighting it out. Even the men in Duran's corner were awed by his courage and amazed at some of the punches he took. For a full two rounds the boxers were like the proverbial immovable object and the irresistible force.

By the sixth round, Sugar Ray was managing to break away from Duran's clutches once in a while, and when he did he made good use of his opportunities, scoring with jabs and left-right combinations. He continued to hold his own through the seventh, eighth, and ninth rounds, but it took every ounce of strength and concentration he could summon. He didn't even notice when, in the eighth round, Juanita fainted. As the rounds continued, Sugar Ray never did gain control of the fight. It was pretty much Duran's the whole way, as they stood head to head and toe to toe, slugging at each other. But Leonard never gave up. Roberto Duran never brought him to his knees. The thirteenth round was the finest of the match. It was extraordinary that either fighter had the strength to get through it, let alone put on such a superb display of boxing skill. As usual, Duran quickly got Leonard into a corner of the ring with a left hook, cutting off the ring, but Leonard just as quickly slipped away. Duran found his mark with another left hook and then dealt Leonard a right. Leonard delivered a right of his own with such force that Duran's head snapped to the side. Then they clutched each other and traded body blows. Leonard's combination of three lefts to the body and two rights to the head were a major factor in his being awarded the round by two of the three judges.

The Panamanian let up in the last two rounds, but not because he was too tired to keep up the pace. Instead, he was still psyching out Sugar Ray Leonard. In the last round, as he jabbed with his left, he tapped his own chin with his right. Then he simply walked away, making "street" gestures questioning Leonard's manhood. Not

Duran won this one.

to be intimidated by Duran, when the final gong sounded, Sugar Ray raised his arms in a victory sign, telling the crowd he believed he had won the fight. Duran rushed up behind him and knocked his hands down. Leonard approached Duran to touch gloves, but Duran refused the glove tap that usually takes place at the end of a bout in which no one has been knocked down.

Although Sugar Ray had put on a confident front as the final bell sounded, he was pretty sure Duran had won. The decision in the Panamanian's favor was unanimous. The French judge had awarded six rounds to Duran, four to Leonard, with five too close to call. The English judge awarded six rounds to Duran, five to Leonard, and four undecided. Only the Italian judge believed that the fighters had been so evenly matched that a full ten rounds were too close to call. Of the other five rounds, he awarded three to Duran and two to Leonard.

Roberto Duran was the new WBC welterweight champion of the world. He was the third man in boxing history to have won the championship in both the lightweight and welterweight classes. Duran had made a lot of money—far more money than he had won in any previous fight. But perhaps most important, the whole world had seen, or would get a chance to see, the Panamanian win. The fight had been carried on closed-circuit television in many places and would be broadcast on commercial television in many other areas. For a man who had grown up as poor as Duran, who'd had to fight on the streets even to survive, this was a sweet victory. He even forgot his animosity toward the man he had beaten. In his locker room after the fight, he was asked by reporters how he felt about Sugar Ray. He yelled back, "Leonard, you're my friend now," but by then Sugar Ray was in his own locker room, out of sight and out of earshot.

If Roberto Duran's victory was sweet, Sugar Ray's loss was bittersweet. In many ways he had done what he had set out to do. He had shown the world that he could indeed take a punch, that he wasn't just a dancer and a prancer without the courage to put his pretty-boy face on the line. He couldn't imagine anyone questioning his courage now. He had met the toughest opponent in the world and shown just as much skill and talent as he had displayed in earlier fights against lesser opponents. Duran may have controlled the fight, but he had never overpowered Sugar Ray. The judges might have awarded the decision unanimously to Duran, but not one of the three had awarded Duran more than two rounds over what he had given Leonard. People were calling the fight a magnificent, memorable combat. That was something for which Leonard could be justly proud. Then, too, there was no taking away the money he had earned from the fight—more than five times what Duran would get—and Sugar Ray Leonard was in the business of boxing for the money.

But Ray had not won, and even a man who approaches the fight game in such a businesslike way cannot help being affected by losing. It was the first time he had lost in his brief professional career. To have lost to someone like Duran didn't make him feel any better. The Panamanian might be a superb fighter, and Leonard was not taking anything away from him for that, but he was the exact opposite of so much that Leonard believed he stood for. In Leonard's eyes, Duran symbolized the side of boxing he didn't like. The fact that raw fury, unsportsmanlike behavior, and macho viciousness had beaten him did not sit at all well with Sugar Ray Leonard.

"What are you going to do now, Ray?" the reporters wanted to know, even before he'd had a chance to shower and have his bruises attended to. Even if he'd had the strength or the desire to answer, Sugar Ray couldn't have, because he didn't know. Most of his plans had depended on a win in Montreal. He was supposed to have been the champion of the world. From that lofty perch he was going to decide whether the product-endorsement offers and all the other opportunities that would go along with it would guarantee him enough money to quit boxing at the top of his class.

But he wasn't champion of anything now. He had lots of money but no title, and his natural pride caused him to dislike the idea of retiring a loser. Then, too, the bruises on his face and the stiffness in his muscles reminded him that to go on in boxing would probably mean more of the same. He did not like what he saw in the mirror. He'd received remarkably few injuries in his career and was not used to seeing physical proof that he had been through a bout. After the Benitez fight, he had been upset because there was discoloration under his eyes and a lump on his forehead, but that was nothing compared to what he saw now.

His whole face was puffy and sore. He had knots on the back of his head. And his left ear was swollen and twisted from Duran's repeated right hooks and from the rubbing of Duran's head against his during the many clinches. Seeing his ear in the mirror, all Sugar Ray could think about were the "cauliflower ears" he'd seen on so many old fighters. That night, so sore that he could barely move, he decided he was a fool to take such abuse any more. "This is it," he told Juanita, and she breathed a sigh of relief.

Juanita had gone to pieces seeing Ray take that punishment from Duran. To her mind, it just wasn't worth it. She didn't want Ray to take further risks, and she was not alone in feeling this way. Mike Trainer agreed with her. He had nurtured Ray's career for four years and enjoyed the experience immensely. But he had not enjoyed seeing Ray in the ring with Duran. Trainer had put Leonard's interests ahead of his own from the very beginning. He held no "percentage" of Sugar Ray Leonard, and so he hadn't that much to lose except maybe his hourly fee if Ray quit. As far as Trainer was concerned, Ray could retire immediately if he wanted to. Dave Jacobs concurred. So did Morton and Dundee. In fact, there wasn't anyone close to Sugar Ray Leonard who had any desire to try to talk him into going on with his fighting career. It was all up to him.

6
SUGAR RAY'S REVENGE

Not long after the Duran match, Sugar Ray and his wife and son took a ten-day vacation to Hawaii as their long-awaited honeymoon. They swam and sunned and walked the beautiful beaches, and gradually the swollen places on Ray's face and the knots on the back of his head, the infection in his ear and the soreness in his body went away. But there was no chance for him to forget his memories of the fight. Everywhere he went he was recognized, and everywhere he went people encouraged him to stay in boxing. "You'll get him next time, champ," they would say. Although they probably did not mean it, Sugar Ray sensed pity in their voices, and if there was one thing he did not want it was pity. His pride would not allow it. He did not want to be pitied for being beaten, especially not by a man like Roberto Duran.

His pride had probably caused him to lose the fight in the first place. The night after the fight, Juanita had asked her husband why he just stood there in the early rounds, letting Duran maul him. Ray had answered that he'd wanted to prove he could take a punch. He didn't want people saying that Duran could have knocked him out if he hadn't spent the whole night running away. Well, he had proved he could take a punch, but he had also lost those early rounds and thus the match.

Ray and Juanita talked about his retiring from the ring. They had enough money to live comfortably for the rest of their lives. The bruises on his face and the knots on the back of his head bothered them both; so did the memory of the strain on Juanita, as she watched her husband get hurt. That didn't ever have to happen again. He need never climb into another ring. But retiring as a loser might be harder to deal with than bruises and knots. People were feeling sorry for him, and neither Ray nor Juanita liked that idea. Ray's own image of himself was that he was a winner, and he wanted to make that image a reality again.

First he had to accept the fact that he had, indeed, lost. He could not do that for a while. A month after the fight, he was insisting that his title had been "confiscated." He'd watched films of the fight and, in his opinion, he had scored more points than Duran. Duran had bulled him and gotten him up against the ropes, but he had connected on more punches, and his punches had been more "clean." He wasn't alone in feeling that way. Some sportswriters agreed with him, and he read and reread their columns.

But most sportswriters and boxing experts thought otherwise, including Sugar Ray's "trainer extraordinaire," Angelo Dundee. Although Dundee thought the officiating in the fight had been lousy, he also believed that Ray had allowed Duran to control the fight. Ray had fought Duran's fight instead of his own. Dundee had warned him against this during training, but Ray had not listened. Dundee and the others who cared about Ray didn't want to say "I told you so." What they wanted was for Ray to accept the loss one way or the other. He should either quit, or stay in the game, but he shouldn't let the loss affect him this way. If he was going to continue to feel that he was robbed, then they hoped he would stay in boxing. Otherwise, he might wind up just like one of those poor old boxers who couldn't talk about anything but their wins and about how they, too, were robbed.

Maybe Sugar Ray Leonard did not fully believe what he was saying. Perhaps he just knew he had to say it. You don't do much for your pride by bad-mouthing yourself. Maybe he had to convince himself that his title had been confiscated in order to psych himself back into the ring. Whatever his reasons, within a month after he lost the welterweight championship, Ray knew he had to win it back—and he knew he had to win it back from Duran. Before his vacation/honeymoon had ended, he told his people that he wanted another chance to fight Duran.

Dundee, Morton, and Trainer were pleased with Ray's decision. They had deliberately refrained from advising him about what to do and were prepared to dismantle the boxing part of Sugar Ray Leonard, Inc., rather than see him continue in boxing without a winning spirit. Now that Ray had regained that winning spirit, they were prepared to back him all the way. No time was wasted in contacting Duran's people. They pooh-poohed the idea of a rematch in the near future. So did Duran. Thanks to the media exposure he'd gotten from the fight against Leonard, the Panamanian was now a "bankable commodity." Why risk another fight against Leonard? A rematch too soon would not generate enough enthusiasm on the part of the public, and so it would not generate enough money. Anyway, WBC rules forbade immediate title rematches, and although such rules could always be waived, it was not customary to have immediate rematches in boxing for a variety of reasons.

For one, other fighters had to be given a chance to fight in important matches. If a boxer had lost the championship, or lost to the champion, he shouldn't get an instant rematch. Someone else should be given the opportunity for a title bout, and the first boxer should step aside and let another fighter have that chance. And then there were the considerations of fan enthusiasm and money that Duran's people had voiced. A title match in boxing is something like the World Series in baseball. A long season, including league play-offs, leads up to the final confrontation between the two teams. By the time the World Series begins, every baseball fan is eager to watch it. If there was a World Series every five or six months, it wouldn't be nearly as exciting as a once-a-year series. The same is true in boxing. Muhammad Ali's three fights with Joe Frazier were spaced over 5 years—in 1971, 1974, and 1975—and 20 months separated the last two.

Sugar Ray did have an alternative. He could try to fight the champion of the WBA welterweight division. Pipino Cuevas and Thomas Hearns were set to vie for that title in the fall, and he could fight the winner of that match. But he wanted to get back into training for something soon. He had already announced that he would return to his gym in New Carrolton in August.

But he didn't want to train for just any fight. He wanted to train for a fight against Duran.

Money has a way of overriding all kinds of logical and even official considerations. Sugar Ray Leonard knew that, and he directed his representatives to press for a rematch. He knew that if Roberto Duran was offered enough money he would consent to a rematch, and if both Leonard and Duran wanted it, the WBC would find a way to bend its rules.

Most of Leonard's people were willing to keep up the pressure, if that's what Ray wanted, and they continued to do so for the next three months. Only Dave Jacobs disagreed. He was not convinced of Ray's ability to beat Duran in an immediate rematch. If Ray lost to Duran again, it would mean the certain end of his career. Why not get some more experience against other boxers? Jacobs suggested. There ought to be at least one warm-up fight before Duran.

Jacobs was overruled, and when he was, he decided it had been one time too many. Saying he could not stay on while Sugar Ray worked for something he did not personally believe in, Jacobs quit the Leonard organization.

Actually, Dave Jacobs had not been happy with his role for a long time. He'd been with Ray from the start. His own wife had cooked dinners to raise money for trips to amateur boxing competitions. He'd trained Ray at the Palmer Park Recreation Center, when the "ring" was just four strips of tape on the basketball court. He'd driven Ray's family and friends to Montreal in a sardine-can van to see Ray win the Olympic gold medal. When Ray had turned pro, he had stayed on in the role of trainer without a contract, because he had an understanding with his young friend. He had profited by their continued relationship, but he had also seen his own influence slip. Angelo Dundee had been hired on as "trainer extraordinaire." People like Trainer and Dundee had taken on more responsibility for making the decisions that affected Sugar Ray's career. Even Janks Morton's influence seemed to become greater than his. Jacobs had kept quiet while Ray worked slowly and steadily toward the welterweight championship; but after Ray beat Wilfredo Benitez and claimed the WBC title, he had spoken up.

He did not demand more influence, because he realized that was futile. Jacobs demanded more money. He told Mike Trainer that he wanted a contract, one that called for 10 percent of Ray's fight earnings. This was in line with what other trainers of established fighters received. Trainer balked. Then Jacobs made public his concerns, and Trainer was furious.

Meanwhile, Sugar Ray Leonard was enjoying a short vacation with Juanita in Las Vegas and California. When he read in the papers about what was happening within his own boxing "family," he stepped in. He and Jacobs met privately, and for a time the difficulties seemed to be resolved. But they were only resolved on the surface. Dave Jacobs still resented his lack of influence on the Leonard "team." He still thought he should be getting more money, and he could not get along at all with Mike Trainer. Jacobs had become the director of Recreation at the Oakcrest Recreation Center in a town near Palmer Park, and he often thought of just devoting all his time to that job. But he still had great regard for Sugar Ray, still felt like a father to him, and he could not pull away. He stayed on through the

Davey "Boy" Green fight, and then through the Duran fight, but after Duran beat Sugar Ray, Dave Jacobs made his decision. He felt like an outsider in the Leonard camp. His opinions were not sufficiently respected; and on top of that, he wasn't getting enough money.

The departure of Jacobs made a crack in the image of Sugar Ray Leonard's "second family," which his fight-business associates had often been called. It seemed as if money and power considerations could drive wedges between even the best of friends, and it bothered Sugar Ray Leonard that this was happening. Jacobs had been like a father to him, and he knew he owed the man a great deal. But he had come a long way since his amateur days. He had new responsibilities. Leonard didn't like the idea that Jacobs had left, but he now had a goal, almost an obsession, that Jacobs could not affect. Besides, there had been times when Jacobs, Morton, and Dundee had disagreed on tactics, and Ray had been confused about whose advice to follow. With Jacobs gone, Morton became solely responsible for Ray's day-to-day training.

Meanwhile, Mike Trainer and others worked at getting that rematch against Duran. Before long Carlos Elcta, Duran's manager, agreed to one. As expected, money was a major consideration. Duran had received only $1.5 million from the earlier fight, and although that seems like a lot of money, it goes quickly when you start doing a lot of spending. Duran's wife, Felicidad, had decided to open a clothing boutique in Panama, and that would take several hundred thousand dollars. And then there were Roberto's expenditures, which were also considerable, for he had many friends and hangers-on.

Another important reason why Eleta wanted the fight was to make Duran get back into training. Duran had put on weight very quickly after the first fight against Leonard. Eleta didn't want him to get too heavy to qualify as a welterweight. It was possible that he could lose his title without ever defending it! So Eleta told Don King to negotiate the terms of a rematch with Mike Trainer. In September, he ordered Duran back into training. At the time Duran weighed 173 pounds.

Don King drove a hard bargain. He was in a position to call the shots this time, because Duran was the champion, not the contender. Even though Duran had won the June 20 bout, he had pocketed only $1.5 million while Leonard took more than $9 million home. This time, Leonard would have to take less. At last it was agreed that, for the rematch, Duran would get $8 million and Leonard $6 million. The only reason Sugar Ray was able to get such a deal was that he could bring the audiences. He was the one who was "box office," even if he had lost to Duran the first time. Don King couldn't argue with that.

On October 2 the official announcement was made. The title rematch was set for the New Orleans Superdome on Tuesday, November 25, 1980. WBC President Jose Sulaiman was on hand to explain that the organization's rule against immediate title rematches had been waived "for the good of boxing." Did anyone believe him?

Ray had really been in training since August, but now intensive training began. Oddly, part of that intensive training, which was now under Morton's auspices completely, was that Ray do *less* work. In the past, he had worked perhaps too long and hard to prepare for a fight. This time Morton wanted him just to keep in shape by running. They went to the training camp in New Carrolton, Maryland, a week later than usual, and even then Ray did not train as hard. While in the past he had sparred as many as 15 rounds a day, every day, this time he sparred no more than 9 rounds in a day. Every so often Morton told him to take a day off. But that is not to say that Ray was not training thoroughly. In terms of strategy, this was the most thorough training session ever.

Heavier sparring partners were brought to the camp at New Carrolton. They were instructed to fight in Duran's style—crowding and mauling Leonard, cutting off the ring and pinning him against the ropes. In response, Ray worked on developing his hand and foot speed inside, in tight situations. He worked to shorten his left hook. Angelo Dundee arrived in November, earlier than usual, to help out with the classroom sessions. Using films of the June 20 fight to emphasize his points, he proved that Duran was not the stupid bull of his reputation. On the contrary, he had a very clever technique. He was constantly doing things to get his opponent off balance—switching his feet, waving his hands, feinting, or pretending to punch with one hand and then landing a blow with the other, grabbing his opponent's head, shoulders, elbows to upset the other man's rhythm. According to Dundee, the only way to deal with these tactics was to counter them with similar moves. Never just stay in front of him, Dundee warned. Never spread your feet so wide that you cannot move quickly. Never back up in a straight line. Do not lie against the ropes. Move from side to side, switch your feet. Feint, too, and as soon as you feel the ropes on your back, spin out. As the night of the fight neared, Dundee would actually get into the ring with Ray and his sparring partner and go through the various positions of arms, feet, and head, step by step.

Sugar Ray Leonard was training to fight smart. He was going to show Duran, and everyone else, that the championship belonged to him. He was going to win so decisively that no one would ever question his abilities again. And this time, *he* was going to psych out Duran. He was going to make Duran look bad, make him crazy.

Another big difference between the Leonard camp in the spring and that in the fall of 1980 was that this time neither Leonard nor his people were talking very much about the upcoming fight. Another prefight "Psych War" might affect Sugar Ray badly. He was not going to get caught up in the hype again.

When the two camps arrived in New Orleans (Duran from a training camp in Miami, Florida, because the weather had gotten too cold for him in the Catskills), Angelo Dundee broke the silence of the Leonard team. A week before the scheduled bout, he publicly expressed his concerns about two things. One was the length of Roberto Duran's beard. Dundee charged that last time Duran had used it as a weapon. He said Leonard's face had shown scratches from the beard. Dundee wanted Duran's beard trimmed. But officials of the WBC and the Louisiana State Athletic Commission didn't think that was called for. Dundee also decided to give the Duran camp some of its own medicine. Last time, Duran's people had made such a fuss over whether the referee would inhibit their fighter that, in Dundee's opinion, they had actually inhibited the referee. This time, Dundee took the offensive. He asked the Louisiana State Athletic Commission to spell out its definition of fouls, such as butting, holding, and grabbing, saying he wanted to make sure its definitions accorded with his.

Butting is using the top of the head to strike the opponent. Dundee said Duran used his head as a weapon so much that maybe they ought to put a glove on it. Holding is just what it says—holding onto an opponent. Dundee said Duran had committed that foul repeatedly when he had Leonard against the ropes in the last fight. Grabbing is another form of holding. By charging that most of Duran's fouls in the first fight had not been called by the referee, Dundee hoped to ensure that the referee on November 25 would be an "active" one.

Sportswriters were glad that Dundee was speaking out. At last someone was! It was hard to write articles about the fight when everyone was being so close-mouthed. The Dundee charges were a new angle. Another angle was the lack of public excitement. Ticket sales were lagging. One obvious reason was that the prices for seats at the New Orleans Superdome were twice as high as they had been for the first fight. But another was the scheduling. Sure, people wanted to see Leonard and Duran meet again, but it takes time to get fan excitement to a fever pitch, no matter how strong their feelings about the boxers or how important the match.

Sugar Ray Leonard didn't much care about the lagging ticket sales. By the agreement he would be fighting for a guaranteed sum, not a percentage. Mike Trainer had insisted on that. He didn't want his business-minded fighter to feel that he had to promote the fight to assure himself a nice profit. But for the first time in his pro career, Ray wasn't in this fight for the money. Win or lose, he would enjoy having it, but he would have fought for $1 if necessary. His pride was at stake in this fight. So was his career. He knew he wouldn't be able to—wouldn't want to—go on in boxing if he lost to Duran in the rematch. What he would do for the rest of his life, and to a great extent how he would feel about himself for the rest of his life, depended on this fight. For this reason, he was again the favorite to win, although not by as much. Favored 9–5 against Duran by Las Vegas odds makers in the first fight, he was a 3–2 favorite this time around.

Motivation is important in competition of all kinds, not just in sports, but of all sports, boxing is probably the one where it is most important. It is man against man, body against body, glove against glove. There are no teammates to help out, no bat or ball or tennis racquet between you and your opponent. All your concentration and energy are focused against a single human being. If you have more motivation than he does, you have an indisputable edge.

Sugar Ray Leonard had motivation that extended beyond considerations of his career and his pride. He had not been able to forget Duran's obscene gestures, the way he had tapped his own jaw with one glove while hitting Leonard with the other, the way he had refused the traditional glove taps. Every time he thought of these things, Ray seethed inside. Part of him actually hated Duran, but he refused to allow that emotion to overpower him. Instead, he used that emotion to increase his determination. Sugar Ray was out for sweet revenge.

There were other reasons behind the odds favoring Leonard. He was five years younger than Duran and thus probably able to bounce back more quickly from the grueling 15-rounder on June 20. Also, he had been back in training longer, following a Spartan regimen while Duran gorged himself on food. But the major factor was motivation. Which fighter could make the better use of the intense dislike he felt for his opponent?

There was much bad will surrounding the rematch, and it wasn't the kind that made for good publicity. If brought together, neither Duran's nor Leonard's people could be sure that the fighters wouldn't start the rematch early. So they were kept apart as much as possible, and when they did have to meet, breaths were held on both sides.

Right after they signed for the second fight, Leonard and Duran filmed a Seven-Up commercial in New York with their two sons. Don King had a talk with Duran and urged him not to taunt Leonard. Everything went smoothly at the filming, possibly because of the presence of the two young boys, but also because neither man wanted to risk losing the money promised if the commercial filming went well.

The two also avoided coming to blows at a prefight press conference, although Duran actually kept his hands tucked under his arms the whole time. Even the official weigh-ins on the day of the fight were accomplished separately. Both men weighed in at exactly 146 pounds. Leonard's weight pleased him. Last time he had weighed in at 144 pounds and had dropped to 140 in the course of the tough contest. With added weight he felt he had added strength. Duran's beard was measured and deemed a suitable length. But it was clear that he'd had to struggle to make weight. He'd been at 160 as recently as the first week in November, and at 148 earlier that very day. Right after his weight was officially taken, he gulped down a thermosful of beef broth and ate two oranges. Everyone around knew what that meant. He was dehydrated, having dieted so strenuously that his body was suffering from a lack of water.

There was one odd occurrence at the weigh-in. Although Leonard arrived at the Superdome first, it was boxing protocol that the champion be the first to be weighed. So Leonard went straight into the room where Dr. A.J. Italiano of the Louisiana State Athletic Commission was waiting to examine both fighters. Meanwhile, Duran arrived and was weighed in, but instead of exchanging places with Leonard and going next to Dr. Italiano, Duran was swept out of the weigh-in room and toward a Superdome exit by his large group of followers, none of whom seemed to understand English. Fortunately, Duran's interpreters arrived and Duran was taken back to the doctor's office. Some people in Leonard's camp charged that the delay was deliberate, that maybe Duran's blood pressure or heart beat were too high. But the doctor pronounced him ready to fight.

Neither fighter was very pleased about the gifts they received that day from Thomas Hearns, now the other welterweight champion of the world (according to the WBA). To show his contempt for both men, Hearns had ordered sent to each—a turkey! For months, Hearns had bad-mouthed Duran and Leonard at every opportunity, primarily to get publicity. He had fully expected that he would be the next opponent of Sugar Ray Leonard and that he would beat him and then beat Duran for the WBC title. When the rematch was announced, he charged that Leonard did not have the guts to fight him and that Duran didn't have the talent.

On the night of November 25, 35,000 people entered the New Orleans Superdome. They did not even fill half of the 79,758 seats, but the atmosphere was lively as they sat through the two preliminary fights. Roger Leonard and Mark Holmes, brother of WBC heavyweight champion Larry Holmes, both took their matches. As ten o'clock neared, the sense of excitement and expectancy of the crowd heightened. They were ready for what had been called "the fight of the decade."

Sugar Ray's entrance delighted them. There had been no sudden loss of will or concentration for Leonard before this fight. He was "up," he felt good, and he was ready. He came down the aisle preceeded by cheerleaders waving pom-poms and chanting, "All the way, Sugar Ray!" Leonard's enthusiastic supporters joined in the chanting. Leonard himself smiled happily and waved to the crowd, but his eyes were deadly serious. Underscoring his determination to be tough this time was the outfit he chose to wear. In the past he had always worn white. For this fight he dressed all in black —black trunks, black socks, and black boxing shoes. Before the fight, he'd asked Mike Trainer how he looked and Trainer had said he looked like the "Grim Reaper." That pleased Sugar Ray. He had wanted to wear an outfit that suggested the aura of an old-time fighter.

Then the champion made his entrance. Salsa music

Sugar Ray taunts Duran—and wins the rematch.

blared and hundreds of small Panamanian flags waved in the air, but the cheering had been louder for Leonard. The pro-Leonard atmosphere was heightened when his namesake, Ray Charles, sang a rousing rendition of "America the Beautiful." Sugar Ray smiled as he listened to the song. He looked relaxed and confident. Duran scowled, but he too looked confident.

The opening bell sounded. Leonard came out circling, moving in and out. Duran was also cautious for the first minute. Then he saw his chance and bulled Leonard to the ropes. But Sugar Ray did not stand and fight. He quickly slipped away and landed the first punch of the bout, a grazing right. They traded quick punches, then Leonard landed a straight left and a hard right to the mouth. Duran smiled. The bell ended the round. As the second round began, Duran immediately bulled Leonard to the ropes, but the referee separated them as they clinched. Ray faked away and laughed. The same thing happened twice more in the round. Sugar Ray wasn't letting Duran control the fight. He was dancing, circling, shifting from side to side, and it seemed to be affecting Duran's timing. The champion missed several shots, and once again at the buzzer Leonard landed two swift jabs.

In the third round Duran regained his timing. He connected with several punches and managed to bull Leonard to the ropes and keep him there, twice. But Ray fought well inside, and neither man was the clear winner of the round. In the fifth round, Sugar Ray slipped to the canvas about the same time Duran landed a right to the body. This was ruled a slip, not a knockdown. The referee wiped off Leonard's gloves. His backside was stained with the resin from the ring floor, but it did not affect his fighting. This round, too, was too close to call.

In the sixth round, Duran seemed continuously short on his jabs, as if his timing was off again. Leonard's were right on the mark. So far, he had controlled the fight, making Duran come after him, and frustrating his opponent's bulling tactics with his constant dancing and circling. The ring floor was in bad shape. A floorboard split in mid-ring. One section, which had sunk down several inches, had probably caused Leonard to slip. After the bell ended the round, that part of the canvas was inspected. Both Ray Arcel and Angelo Dundee tested the sinking area and agreed that the fight should not be delayed because of it. In round seven, as Leonard and Duran fought, workmen attempted to repair the ring from underneath.

Duran again regained his timing in the seventh round. Right off, he landed a hook to the head and another to the stomach and pushed Leonard to the ropes. Leonard answered with a jab to the body. He had been dancing around throughout the fight. Now he began to taunt Duran, dancing and circling but not throwing any punches. Duran scowled. He did not like clowning. Leonard was acting like Muhammad Ali, and Duran was not the only one who made that comparison. Leonard continued to dance and suddenly, in amazement, he realized that Duran was watching his feet. "I've got him now," Leonard said to himself.

As if in confirmation, the voice of Howard Cosell, who was doing ringside commentary, came through to him. "Duran is completely bewildered!" exclaimed Cosell.

Still taunting, Sugar Ray wound up his right arm as if to throw a bolo, then suddenly changed and came out with a left that struck Duran square in the face and made his eyes water. There were hoots of laughter from the crowd. Then Sugar Ray opened his eyes wide in pretended fright and stood flat-footed, jutting his chin out, daring Duran to take his best shot. He went into the Ali Shuffle, moving his shoulders from side to side, arms dangling at his sides. He faked a windup with his right arm and motioned for Duran to come to him. Sneering, Duran bulled him to the ropes with body punches. Then the two went at it along the ropes in a furious exchange of punches.

At the start of the eighth round the referee decided there was too much Vaseline on Duran's body and insisted on toweling some of it off. When the fight resumed, Leonard began moving from side to side, flicking jabs at Duran. Like a bull after a wily matador, Duran charged at his opponent and tried to force him to the ropes. Leonard backed up and scored a hard right to the jaw. He then landed two left jabs and a left-right-left combination that staggered his opponent. With about one minute left in the round, Leonard had Duran backed into the ropes. Suddenly Duran dropped his hands to his sides and said, *"No más"*—no more.

It took the startled Sugar Ray only an instant to realize what that meant. Duran didn't want to fight any more. He, Sugar Ray, was the winner. He leapt into the air in triumph.

The Mexican referee, Octavio Meyran, would not hear of Duran's quitting. He signaled Leonard to continue fighting. Sugar Ray turned and delivered a hard left-right combination to Duran's body. Duran didn't even try to defend himself. He kept his hands at his sides. *"No más,"* he said again. This time the referee did not try to overrule Duran. At 2 minutes and 44 seconds into the eighth round of a scheduled 15-round fight, it was official: With a technical knockout, Sugar Ray Leonard was once again the WBC welterweight champion. Curiously enough, Duran, who had refused to touch gloves with Leonard in Montreal, now embraced the new champion before he left the ring—but not before Roger Leonard had leapt into the ring and thrown a punch at him.

A stunned silence fell over the crowd in the Superdome. Then there was an uneasy buzz as people asked each other, "What happened?" As recognition that the fight was over dawned on everyone, the reactions understandably varied. Some cheered Leonard. Others booed Duran. And many shouted "Fix! Fix!" Never before, in all of boxing history, had a champion walked away from his title so unexpectedly and inexplicably. Never had there been a more bizarre ending to a title bout. And never in the world would anyone who knew boxing have believed that Roberto Duran would just quit. Why, he'd sooner die in the ring—or so everyone thought.

Muhammad Ali had once continued fighting with a broken jaw. Henry Armstrong had gulped down blood for five rounds after a referee said that he would stop the fight if Armstrong kept bleeding. There was a time, back in 1949, when middleweight champion Marcel Cerdan was forced to quit with a pulled muscle in his right shoulder and Jake LaMotta had been awarded the title; but Cerdan had had a definite injury. Roberto Duran looked fine. In the confusion after the Superdome fight ended, there were rumors that Duran had cramps in his stomach, in his legs and arms, and that he had a separated shoulder. But doctors who examined him after the fight could find absolutely nothing wrong with him.

So why had Duran quit? Speculation was rampant, but there was no clear answer. He had fought a good fight. At the end of the seventh round, two of the three judges had scored Leonard ahead four rounds to two, with one round tied, and the third judge had scored them even closer, four rounds to three. Duran could have pulled himself together and won—he had seven more rounds in which to do it.

Some people suggested that the real reason Duran quit was his extreme macho self-image. Leonard had teased him, taunted him, and caused him to lose face. Like the typical neighborhood bully, he could not take such insults. When he couldn't shut Leonard up with his fists, he didn't want to play any more.

In his locker room after the fight, Duran informed his associates and friends that he was retiring from boxing. Even those who were the loudest to yell "Quitter!" couldn't help seeing the sad aspect of what had happened. Duran, who had won 72 of 74 fights, 41 straight victories, scored 55 knockouts, and had 13 successful title fights, would be remembered best for the one fight that he walked out on.

Life was not going to be easy for Roberto Duran. Although, strangely enough, he had a party in his locker room after the fight was over, he realized that his name was going to be mud in his native country. He had planned to fly from New Orleans to New York with his wife and son. Orders to cancel those plans and return immediately to Panama soon came, directly from General Omar Torrijos, Panama's president. Roberto Duran, being the number one national hero, was also something of a national possession. It would be very difficult for him in Panama. It was a small country—only about two million people lived there. Everyone knew him. There would be no place to hide.

Over in his locker room, Sugar Ray Leonard avoided criticizing Duran. As champion, he could of course afford to be sympathetic, but there was more to his reticence than that. Leonard realized that something had to be very wrong with Duran, be it mental or physical, to cause him to walk away from the fight. Despite his intense personal dislike of Duran, Sugar Ray had always respected him as a fighter. Leonard's idea of good sportsmanship did not include kicking a man when he was down. Angelo Dundee felt the same way. He objected to the word *quitter* as applied to Duran. Try as they might, sportswriters got no words of rancor from the Leonard camp, only happiness and celebration.

Still, there was a slight shadow over Sugar Ray's happy feelings about regaining the championship. He would have preferred winning it decisively—by a knockout, or at least by a technical knockout after the full 15 rounds. He knew he had proved that he could control the fight and make Duran box his way and that he was a better fighter than Duran. But he did not like the idea of a victory surrounded by so much controversy. Still, he was the victor and had regained the championship, and so when Thomas Hearns threw a rubber chicken at him after the fight, he did not stop to respond. It was just Hearns trying to get more publicity. He would respond to the rubber chicken as well

128

as to the live turkey when he met Hearns in the ring.

Later on, after the full impact of what had happened really sank in, Leonard began to see his bizarre victory in a different light—as the sweetest kind of victory to have. He had *made* Duran quit. He had done just what he had set out to do. He made Duran mad, made him crazy, so crazy that he had to quit. To make a man like Roberto Duran quit was even better than knocking him out.

Ordinarily after a championship fight the winner gets more publicity than the loser. But the November 25 fight at the New Orleans Superdome had been no ordinary fight. If they weren't bemoaning the state of boxing, sportswriters were more likely to write about Roberto Duran than Sugar Ray Leonard.

Their concern about the state of boxing was justified. During 1980 there had been two major fights that had been downright embarrassing. Earlier in the year, Muhammad Ali had come out of retirement yet again to meet heavyweight champion Larry Holmes in Las Vegas. The fight had been scheduled for 15 rounds, and the 38-year-old Ali stood up gamely for 10 of them. But he had taken a terrible pounding and his people would not let him go out for the eleventh. Later, Ali admitted to having taken an overdose of weight-reducing drugs and being weak and dehydrated as a result. People had paid high prices to see that fight live or on closed-circuit television, and understandably they had felt cheated. Then came the Leonard-Duran fight, and this time the fans didn't just feel cheated, they felt downright hood-winked. People who cared about the sport of boxing worried that many fans would just get disgusted with the game and cease to be fans at all. Something had to be done to ensure that such things would not happen again.

There was a brief attempt to withhold Duran's share of the fight purse, but there was no way to do that legally. Instead, Duran was fined $7,500 for not performing up to WBC standards. WBC officials decided to look into the matter of stiffer fines, but for the time being all anyone could do was hope that the two embarrassing fights in the same year were flukes. Two days after the Superdome bout, boxing was embarrassed even more when Roberto Duran declared that he had decided not to retire after all and wanted a rematch.

"Sure, when hell freezes over" was the response of most people in boxing. Duran had dashed any chance of ever being considered a serious boxer again. Still, it bothered just about everyone not to have a clear answer about why he had quit in the ring, and so there was much newspaper space devoted to the possible reasons. The one true answer could only come from Duran himself, and he was not talking. Although there was evidence that Duran might not have been completely well physically, that he might have had problems with his heart or blood pressure and that he most assuredly had been forced to diet much too strenuously to "make weight," the general consensus of opinion was that his real problem had been hurt pride. Sugar Ray Leonard, the man whom Duran had psyched out even before the Montreal fight began, had subjected him to the most sustained humiliation he had ever suffered. Duran simply could not take it for another seven rounds. So, he had chosen to dismiss Leonard: "If you won't come in and fight like a man . . ." But his strategy had backfired. The macho men saw no strength in that. They only saw a quitter.

7
CHAMPION OF THE WORLD

It took Sugar Ray Leonard quite some time to come down from the "high" of his fight with Roberto Duran. He had concentrated so intensely on winning that life seemed suddenly empty and purposeless. But that was often how he felt after a fight, and he did not let it worry him. He knew that he would soon be back in training. He determined to make the most of this in-between time when boxing did not have to be the most important thing in his life.

He went on long walks with Juanita. She liked to say that taking a walk in the park helped to put things into perspective, that seeing the beauty of Nature made people's problems seem smaller, and, for that matter, their triumphs seem smaller, too. Walking in the park, Sugar Ray realized that beating Roberto Duran had not been such an earth-shaking event. The world seemed to be going along pretty much as before.

He also spent a lot of time with Little Ray, mostly playing basketball, softball, and football. Occasionally he sparred with his son. Although Ray, Jr., was only seven, he did not want to be a boxer. In the small boy's opinion, you could get hurt in boxing. He did not like seeing his father fight any more than his mother did. He wanted his father to beat Thomas Hearns and then quit the ring.

Mike Trainer had other ideas. He realized that Sugar Ray would have to meet Hearns at some point, but he did not want it to be too soon. He wanted Ray to have time to take advantage of all his opportunities both to make money and to develop as a fighter, and he was devising a plan that would do just that. The plan took into account the WBC rule that a champion must defend his title three times a year against one of the top ten contenders—and Ray saw it as a chance to gain a special place in boxing history.

Step one called for Leonard to meet Larry Bonds in Syracuse, New York, at the end of March. Bonds, a 29-year-old sanitation worker from Denver, was an unknown. He had not even fought for a year. But Trainer was not looking for a *fight* between Leonard and Bonds. As he put it, their meeting would be "an event." Trainer wanted to show that Sugar Ray could fight a virtual unknown in a small city and still draw a crowd. He claimed that people would pay to see Sugar Ray perform under any circumstances.

Syracuse was not a stranger to prize fighting. Years before, it had hosted some major fights with such contenders as Carmen Basilio and the DeJohn brothers. But there hadn't been a title fight in Syracuse since Billy Backus had beaten José Napoles for the welterweight crown 11 years before. Not surprisingly, Syracuse rolled out the red carpet for Sugar Ray Leonard, and he responded with equal grace, making a number

of publicity appearances and signing hundreds of auto-
graphs every day. Angelo Dundee announced that
Sugar Ray would display in Syracuse a new punch—"a
Carmen Basilio uppercut, with either hand." And
finally, tickets for this bout were going to be priced with
the "little people" in mind. The top price would be $60,
and only 15 percent of the tickets would be that expensive. The other 85 percent would be $20 and $10. These
prices were a far cry from the $500 and $1000 ringside
seat prices at Montreal and New Orleans.

Leonard would not make much from live gate receipts, but Trainer expected him to net about three-
quarters of a million dollars from cable-television
broadcasts of the fight.

As expected, Leonard easily defeated Bonds in the
ten-round bout. But 21,000 people filled Syracuse's new
domed arena to see him, and thousands more watched
the fight on cable TV. Added to that, 6,000 spectators,
many of them children, had attended Leonard's six
prefight workouts in Syracuse. Mike Trainer kept track
of these attendance figures. He planned to use them
when negotiating terms for the really big fights that lay
ahead—against Thomas Hearns or middleweight
champion Marvin Hagler, or the man whom Hearns
had beaten for the WBA welterweight championship,
Pipino Cuevas. If Leonard could draw that many spectators for a fight against a sanitation worker from Denver, just think of how many people would pay to see
him against a world-ranked opponent.

Trainer and Dundee had another reason for choosing
Larry Bonds for the bout in Syracuse. He is a left-
hander. Leonard had not fought a left-hander since
beating Adolfo Viruet and Tony Chiaverini two years

before. He needed practice, for Marvin Hagler is a left-hander.

Ayub Kalule was chosen as the opponent in Leonard's next fight. He is right-handed, but he fights like a left-hander. Leonard would not defend his title against Kalule. On the contrary, Leonard was going to be the challenger in this bout, for Kalule was the WBA junior middleweight champion.

Weight for junior middleweight boxers is 154 pounds. Sugar Ray Leonard would have no trouble making that weight. In fact, it was clear that he would soon have to move out of the welterweight class. At 24, Sugar Ray Leonard was still growing. He had grown a half inch taller in the past year. There was new muscular growth in his neck and thighs, and it was certain that his muscularity would only increase. He would be a middleweight before long. In the meantime, he had the opportunity to experiment in the higher weight class. Just possibly, he could hold two titles—welterweight and junior middleweight—simultaneously.

Ayub Kalule, who lives in Denmark, is a Ugandan of the Baganda tribe. The 26-year-old had been unbeaten in all 36 of his previous fights, scoring knockouts in exactly half of them. Although he was not known in the United States, he was respected in international boxing circles as a fine man and a powerful, though not brilliant, fighter. No one expected him to be able to beat Leonard, but he would be a worthy opponent. The match was scheduled for June 21 in the Houston Astrodome.

Meanwhile, Mike Trainer and Angelo Dundee had arranged for Leonard to meet Thomas Hearns, in the fight the boxing world had been waiting for, on September 16, 1981, in Las Vegas, Nevada. A Hearns fight "on the same card" as Leonard in June would promote the September bout. Thus, on April 27, two days after Hearns successfully defended his WBA welterweight title against Randy Shields, it was announced that in Houston, on the same night as Leonard met Kalule, Hearns would fight Pablo Baez, a Dominican fighter.

Emanuel Steward, Hearns's manager and trainer, wanted the Hearns-Baez fight to be last, but he changed his mind when Mike Trainer pointed out that the media wouldn't give the last fight much coverage —the reporters would be too busy interviewing Sugar Ray Leonard. As it turned out, there wasn't much of a Hearns-Baez fight to watch.

Bob Arum volunteered to promote the Leonard-Kalule fight. One of his press agents, Irving Rudd, decided that a good way to get publicity would be to capitalize on Kalule's Ugandan tribal background. He would bring in a witch doctor! Not knowing any witch doctors personally, Rudd called the Ugandan Mission to the United Nations in New York City. Someone there put him in touch with Ben Mugimba, a witch doctor who claimed he could make rain, stop a tornado, and put curses on people. He was also a Catholic with six children who once operated a gas station in Kampala, the capital of Uganda. He was presently running a coffee plantation in that country. Mugimba was flown to the United States to summon the support of the spirits for Kalule and put a few curses on Sugar Ray Leonard.

When Sugar Ray heard about the witch doctor, he laughed. Recognizing that it was a publicity stunt, he decided to play along. He sent someone to the library to research Ugandan witch doctors. When he learned that witch doctors fear the color black and don't like snakes because they are too quick moving to put a spell on, Leonard ordered a special outfit for the fight. This outfit included a black robe with yellow serpents on the sleeves and black trunks with a yellow cobra on the left leg!

The witch-doctor publicity stunt was short-lived. Ayub Kalule did not laugh when he was introduced to Ben Mugimba. He was insulted. Charging that Rudd must think him a fool, he reminded everyone that he did not just come out of the jungle. So, no curses were put on Sugar Ray Leonard, but he wore his anti witch-doctor outfit on fight night anyway.

In Houston, Thomas Hearns took care of Pablo Baez easily, in the fourth round of a scheduled ten-round fight. It would hardly have been a fitting climax to a big fight card.

Then Sugar Ray Leonard and Ayub Kalule squared off for their 15-round bout. It was expected that Leonard would dance around the ring and force Kalule to come after him, but he surprised just about everyone by going right after the Ugandan with lightning-quick jabs. For two full rounds Kalule seemed unable to defend himself from those jabs. Then, in the third round, Leonard threw a left hook to Kalule's head and injured his own middle finger. He had suffered the same injury several times before. It would cause him pain any time he jabbed at his opponent's head but would not hinder a hook to the softer target of Kalule's body. Still, the injury clearly handicapped him. His left jab was the trigger for all his combination punches.

To compensate, Sugar Ray came out roaring in the

fourth round. The flurry of punches caused Kalule to lose his balance four times, but he did not go down. Kalule was known as an iron man. He never had been knocked down, and it didn't look as if Ray Leonard was going to be able to do it.

In the next round Kalule began to find his rhythm, and midway in the seventh round he knocked Leonard off balance with a right to the head that actually spun Sugar Ray around. Suddenly, it looked as if the careful plan might crumble. What if Sugar Ray lost to Kalule? What if experimenting in a higher weight class turned out to be a mistake? As Kalule appeared to gain even more confidence in the eighth round, a foul-up in Trainer's careful plan seemed all too possible.

Then, in the ninth round, Kalule fell apart. With his left hand demanding a break, Leonard unleashed everything he had with his right. Two hard punches to the head drove him to the corner, but Leonard got off two solid rights before Kalule could get away. Leonard went after his opponent, and with another right he put Kalule back against the ropes. Leonard then unleashed two savage left-right combinations, and Ayub Kalule, who had never before been knocked down, found himself on the floor. The referee, Carlos Berrocal, began the count. Kalule was on his feet by the count of six, but he was dazed. Berrocal asked if he was all right and Kalule shook his head, no. The referee gave the signal and the fight was over. Leonard had won with a technical knockout.

Sugar Ray had been practicing a special acknowledgment of his win. He leapt into the air now and did a no-hands flip that delighted the crowd. It was the perfect finish to an interesting and well-fought bout, and a fitting reaction for a man who now held both the WBC welterweight and the WBA junior middleweight titles.

Suddenly the attention of the boxing world shifted completely to the upcoming Leonard-Hearns fight. Houston had generated excitement primarily because people had a chance to make judgments about how Leonard and Hearns would do against each other. Now it was if boxing fans—and the fighters themselves— were saying, "Well, now that's over with. On to the big one." Representatives of both fighters had agreed that the bout would be described in the contract the two signed only as a 15-round welterweight fight. No title was mentioned. They feared that one of the world boxing organizations might try to create trouble. This fear was well-grounded. Sugar Ray Leonard was in a unique position. He held the WBC welterweight championship, and there was no problem with that. But in beating Ayub Kalule he had also gained the WBA junior middleweight title, and the WBC has rules against holding two titles in different organizations at the same time. Everyone involved hoped to iron out these potential problems over the next couple of months, so the Leonard-Hearns fight could indeed be a bout to unify the welterweight title, but they thought it best to leave all mention of titles out of the contract.

The contract called for Leonard to earn at least $8 million and Hearns $5 million. This was because, although they were both champions of equal importance, Leonard was clearly recognized as the bigger drawing card. But written into the contract were two stipulations. Half the advertisements for the fight would call it the Leonard-Hearns match and the other half the

Hearns-Leonard match. Also, when fight night came, a coin would be flipped to see who entered the ring first.

Both fighters realized that if they could attract a large live audience and a huge cable-television audience, they stood to get much more money than the contract called for. Within two weeks after the June 21 bouts, the hyping of the September 16 fight began. Actually, there wasn't anyone involved who worried about staging a fight and having no one come. Sugar Ray Leonard and Thomas Hearns were the two most exciting fighters in their weight class, if not in the game, and the public had been anxious for a showdown for months and months. Even Sugar Ray stated publicly that this was one fight that needed no hype. So why didn't he just keep quiet and train instead of appearing at all those press conferences and saying bad things about Hearns? He did so not so much to hype the fight as to psych Hearns.

Leonard had no illusions about beating Hearns, whose nickname was "The Hitman." The Detroiter was tough and clever, and he had important physical advantages. At 6'1" tall, Hearns had three inches in height over Leonard, and his reach was four inches longer. Besides, he was three years younger.

Hearns had no illusions about Leonard either. Leonard had the experience of having gone through big-fight hoopla, not just once but twice, against Roberto Duran. Hearns realized Sugar Ray would try to use that advantage, would try to psych him and make him get caught up in the hype. He insisted that Ray would not psych him out.

Hearns is not charismatic like Sugar Ray, and at first he did not try to be. He had nothing bad to say about

Leonard, he said. But he also warned that, like everyone else, he had a boiling point. Leonard, he said, should not want him to reach it.

Although Thomas Hearns did not come across as apple-pie nice the way Sugar Ray did, he, too, was a good person, kind of shy, a family man. Born in Memphis, Tennessee, in 1959, Hearns grew up in Detroit. His father left the family when Thomas was young, and he and his seven brothers and sisters were raised by their mother. They were poor but proud, and Thomas managed to escape the enticements of crime and drugs by devoting most of his nonschool hours to boxing at the Kronk Recreation Center. He started boxing at the age of 11, when he was a scrawny 55 pounds. With the help of Emanuel Steward, the center's boxing trainer, he worked his way up in the amateur ranks. Although he and Ray Leonard, who was three years older, were not often on the same national teams, they did meet each other through amateur boxing. Hearns won both the Golden Gloves and the national AAU titles in 1977 and turned pro in November of the same year. Sitting at ringside and cheering him on for his first professional fight, which he won by a knockout, was none other than Sugar Ray Leonard.

Hearns personally liked Leonard, and Leonard liked Hearns. The rubber chicken–throwing incident after the second Leonard-Duran fight and the live-turkey gifts to Leonard and Duran before that fight had not been Hearns's ideas, but those of a misguided public-relations man. In boxing, you see, opponents are not supposed to like each other. They are *supposed* to say rotten things about each other. Hearns would learn to play the game in time.

Construction of a huge, 25,000-seat temporary boxing arena began in a tennis court adjacent to Caesar's Palace in Las Vegas. Arrangements were made by the promoters of the fight for on-site ticket selling, 300 closed-circuit TV sites, and nearly 20 cities on pay television (the first time ever for a major sporting event). One of the lesser promoters, but still a long way from his term paper days, was Dan Doyle, who had promoted some of Leonard's earliest pro fights. He had the New England closed-circuit TV rights with his partner for the venture, Shelly Finkel, a rock music promoter. Actually, Doyle had tried to promote a Leonard-Hearns bout all by himself back in 1978, but Leonard's people had suggested they wait. Now, Doyle was very glad they had. Back then he was going to offer Leonard $100,000 and Hearns $12,000, hoping to make a few thousand himself. Now, even with just half of the New England closed-circuit TV rights, he stood to make much, much more. It promised to be the richest fight in boxing history.

At this relatively early stage, people who really knew boxing were about evenly divided on who would win. Those who favored Hearns pointed to his height and reach advantages, his superb right jab, and how he had fought against Pipino Cuevas to capture the WBA welterweight title in the summer of 1980. Cuevas had never been beaten, never even been knocked off his feet or visibly hurt; yet Hearns had knocked him out cold midway in the second round.

Those who favored Leonard pointed to his intelligence, his ability to learn with every new fight, to adjust to his opponents. They also considered him by far the more experienced fighter when it came to big tests.

Hearns had defended his title three times since winning it from Cuevas. He had knocked out Luis Primera in the sixth round on December 6, 1980, and on April 25, 1981, he'd had a technical knockout against Randy Shields. He'd beaten Baez in Houston. But none of these competitors even approached the power of someone like Roberto Duran.

Meanwhile, Ray Leonard and Thomas Hearns were in training. As usual, sparring partners were chosen for Ray on the basis of how much they were like his future opponent. They were taller and had longer reaches.

These requirements excluded Odell Leonard, who had been one of Ray's sparring partners on a fairly regular basis since 1974. Many people had assumed that Odell was Ray's cousin, but actually he was no relation at all. Odell Leonard was really Odell Davis, a native of North Carolina who had come under Dave Jacobs's wing in 1974 and after a fairly good amateur career had turned pro. Now, he was one of the fighters Jacobs managed. He had changed his last name to Leonard after Sugar Ray had won the Olympic gold medal, hoping to capitalize on the famous name. Ray Leonard had not known what to think about that; he had been both flattered and annoyed. But he had let it pass.

When Odell Leonard was turned down as Ray's sparring partner for the Hearns fight, he went to the Hearns camp and was hired. Some assistants to Emanuel Steward, Hearns's trainer, were worried that Odell was really a spy for Leonard, but they stopped worrying when they learned that Odell was no relation to Ray and that he was angry at being turned down as Ray's sparring partner. Also hired as a sparring partner for Hearns was Lloyd Taylor, another of Jacobs's fighters. But the big news was that Dave Jacobs had also joined Hearns's camp.

Dave Jacobs and Emanuel Steward had been friends since both had coached U.S. amateur boxing teams. Jacobs had worked with Hearns as an amateur, just as Steward had worked with Leonard when he was an amateur. In late July 1981, Hearns and his entourage went to Palmer Park on a prefight publicity tour. At the Palmer Park Recreation center, Steward asked Jacobs to join the Hearns team. Jacobs accepted.

When they heard about it, Sugar Ray and the rest of his camp were angry. Janks Morton told reporters that Ray had paid for Jacobs's house and two cars, besides putting a lump sum in his bank account. What kind of thanks was it to join the camp of Ray's opponent? Ray himself did not comment publicly on the matter, but even after his anger subsided he was hurt by the action of the man to whom he had been so close for so many years.

Jacobs bore no ill will against Ray, and he had mixed feelings about taking the job. He wasn't quite sure what he was supposed to do as a member of Hearns's team. He knew Emanuel Steward did not need any help training Hearns. He realized he could be useful because he knew so much about Leonard, but he also realized that his main value would be psychological. Sugar Ray was trying to psych out Hearns with words. The presence of Jacobs in the opposite corner of the ring was obviously calculated to psych out Leonard.

By September the Leonard-Hearns/Hearns-Leonard bout, called just a welterweight match in their contract, was being touted as a match to unify the welterweight title. The various potential problems with the WBA and the WBC had been ironed out. Not since Roberto Duran had knocked out Esteban DeJesus on January 21, 1978, to consolidate the WBA and WBC lightweight titles had there been any other unification. For various reasons, this consolidation of titles in September 1981 was not expected to last long, but it was one more reason for excitement over the match. An even greater cause for excitement was how evenly matched the two fighters were. When betting on the fight opened in Las Vegas, Leonard was an 8 to 5 favorite, but that was primarily because he was better known. As fight night approached, Hearns was favored 7 to 5. Few bettors made their wagers with certainty. Sportswriters and sportscasters were compelled to chose either Leonard or Hearns, but nearly all admitted that the fight could go either way.

Still, more experts picked Hearns and the reasons were boringly familiar to Sugar Ray. He'd had it too easy. He'd never really been hurt. He'd never been knocked down in a pro fight and according to boxing wisdom until a fighter is knocked down even he does not know how he will react to the shock and the embarrassment of it. No one knew if Sugar Ray had the will to stay in there and fight if he were hurt. They were not sure if, as sportswriter Dave Anderson put it, he had "the soul of a gladiator." (Anderson picked Hearns to knock out Leonard in the fifth round; most others who favored Hearns thought the fight would go at least 12 rounds.)

It was all very exasperating for Sugar Ray. What did he have to do to prove himself—get killed? Had everyone forgotten the Benitez fight, the first Duran fight? He'd gotten hurt in those bouts hadn't he? Wasn't questioning about his toughness getting kind of dog-eared? Ray was beginning to think that people were not ever going to take him seriously because of his "pretty" face and all-American image. Well, he was not going to get hurt just to prove he could take it. He was going to beat Hearns through artistry, go inside and deprive his opponent of the advantage of that long reach, get him confused, hit him in the body, and knock him flat.

On the night of September 16, every single seat at the temporary arena adjacent to Caesar's Palace was filled. The seats had been sold within days of the stadium's completion. Hollywood stars, stars who were appearing at the various casinos, stars from the athletic world, and just about every top-ranked American boxer, as well as former champions like Muhammad Ali and Joe Frazier and Sugar Ray Robinson, were there, sweltering in the 100-degree heat of the early desert evening. As provided for by contract, there had been a coin flip to decide who would enter the ring first. Sugar Ray had won and had elected to enter last. Hearns entered the ring to cheers and applause. His robe bore the legend "Winner Take All," which was a reference to his prefight statements that he would take away Leonard's title *and* his Seven-Up commercial. At his request, he was introduced as the "Motor City Cobra." Sugar Ray then arrived to cheers and applause of equal volume. The back of his robe read "Deliverance," which was a reference to his being tired of having Hearns around as a challenger.

The three judges, all Las Vegas men, were introduced. The referee, Davey Pearl, outlined the rules of the fight. If a fighter was knocked down, he had to take a mandatory eight count; a fighter could not be saved by the bell except in the fifteenth round; scoring would be on the ten-point system, with the winner of a round getting ten points and the loser anything below that. Sugar Ray Leonard and Thomas Hearns tapped gloves, the opening bell sounded, the crowd roared, and the fight between two perfectly matched athletes began. It was too close to call.

In the early rounds, Sugar Ray concentrated on defense. He danced, he moved from side to side. He shook his hips and smiled as Hearns pursued him with his long jabs. On occasion, he threw a jab or released a combination, but he threw comparatively few punches in the first five rounds. His strategy was to tire Hearns. Hearns had never gone more than ten rounds in one bout. Also, Hearns had weighed in at 145 pounds, 2 pounds lighter than the legal limit. The 100-degree temperature in Las Vegas was augmented another 20 degrees in the ring by the television lights. Both fighters were perspiring furiously, but Hearns had been underweight to begin with. Sugar Ray hoped that he would grow tired and weak quickly. The only problem for Sugar Ray was his left eye, which had been hurt in a sparring session two weeks earlier. In the early rounds, Hearns hit the wound, and by the beginning of the fourth round it had started to swell. Sugar Ray tried not to worry, but he realized it could continue to swell and hamper his vision.

Angelo Dundee was prepared for the eye problem. A few months earlier he'd learned about a small steel object that was effective against swelling. He said it was like a little iron. Between rounds, he pressed the instrument against the swollen spot, but of course it did not work miracles. The eye was still injured. A change of tactics was in order. As the sixth round began, Leonard started on the attack. He missed a left but scored with a right to his opponent's jaw. Hearns came back with two jabs to Leonard's face. They traded punches for a minute. Then Leonard scored with two left-right combinations. At the bell Hearns was visibly hurt. He was still hurt as the seventh round began, and Leonard stopped dancing to size up his opponent's condition. Then he attacked with his left. Hearns wobbled. He struck back with his right jab. Leonard answered with a furious combination that drove Hearns to the ropes. More combinations from Leonard. Hearns looked as if he had lost all strength. But he fought back and landed a couple of powerful punches to Leonard's body before the round ended.

By the eighth round, both men were tired. With his left eye swelling, Sugar Ray was clearly looking to end the fight. He stalked Hearns, and now it was Hearns who began to dance and move from side to side on defense. When Leonard hit him, he just smiled. Incredibly, they had switched styles completely! The puncher was now the dancer, and vice versa.

In Leonard's corner, Angelo Dundee used his little iron and an ice pack to control the swelling near his fighter's left eye. In the ninth round, Leonard again went on the attack, but Hearns seemed to have recovered completely. Looking fresher than Leonard, he concentrated his jabs at that injured eye, which began to swell again.

Both men took a rest in the tenth round, doing more dancing than punching. The crowd booed the fighters, especially Leonard, who had ceased his aggressive attack. In the eleventh, Hearns was the aggressor, scoring repeatedly with lefts and rights, especially his famous jab. His supporters began to chant "Tom-ee, Tom-ee," and between rounds he jumped up from his stool and acted as cheerleader. Hearns was unmarked. Over in the opposite corner, Leonard's eye was closing fast.

Leonard tried to regroup in the twelfth round. He scored with a left and started to dance. Hearns stalked him, landing a left jab and hurting him with another right. There were no smiles now. Leonard took three more right jabs from Hearns before landing a good left that drove Hearns backward. Then Hearns scored a vicious left to the damaged eye as the round ended. For a second the two fighters just looked at each other. Then they tapped gloves. It was a signal of mutual respect. Whoever won, both were giving it everything they had.

Between rounds, Leonard's people worked feverishly on his eye. "You're blowing it, kid, you're blowing it!" yelled Dundee, and Sugar Ray knew he was right. He was tired, worried, and his fighting showed it. He was going to lose unless he could summon his will to fight on and win. Vision blurred, body aching, he reached deep down inside himself and brought up the guts, the will, that many had questioned even existed.

The opening bell rang and Sugar Ray bounced into the ring. He quickly landed a left jab but was short with a right. Hearns stumbled, but the referee ruled it was not a knockdown. Ray continued his attack, driving a right to the body and scoring with two lefts. Hearns countered with a right jab and a right jab–left hook combination. Leonard threw a wild punch and took two more of Hearns's lefts in his face. Then Ray threw a vicious right that connected. Hearns staggered, lost his balance, and fell backward between the ropes. Again, the referee ruled no knockdown. Hearns got back into the ring and threw a hard right, but Leonard scored with a left hook and a right. Hearns wobbled. Leonard moved in for the kill with a big left hook, two rights, and another left. Hearns lay between the ropes again. This time it was ruled a knockdown. Hearns took a standing eight count. Then the round ended.

In the corner, Dundee was telling Sugar Ray to put Hearns away. By now his left eye was little more than a slit the width of a dime. As the opening bell sounded, Sugar Ray charged across the ring and banged away at Hearns's head. Hearns, still dazed, clutched Leonard. They backed away from one another and Hearns landed a jab, but there was little power in it. Leonard threw a hard left to the body, then a powerful right, then a series of rights, then another left hook, then a hard left-right combination. Hearns went down. The referee stopped the fight. It was 1 minute and 45 seconds into the fourteenth round.

Later, some people would criticize the referee's action, saying he should have let the two fight it out to the end. But Davey Pearl had looked down at Thomas Hearns and seen not just a fighter but a 22-year-old man, and he didn't think that young man could be hit any more.

Sugar Ray Leonard had won! He hugged his brother Roger, Janks Morton, and Angelo Dundee. He waved to the cheering crowd. He could hardly see out of his left eye, but at the moment that didn't bother him. He had shown everyone who questioned his will, questioned his guts. Now, there could be no more questions.

After they had showered and had their injuries seen

to, Sugar Ray Leonard and Thomas Hearns appeared together at a postfight press conference. With Little Ray sitting at his side and his wife and mother standing behind him, Sugar Ray beamed. His dark glasses hid the worst injury he had ever received in a fight. Despite the pain and his not inconsiderable vanity, he was elated. It was the toughest fight he had ever fought, he told the reporters, and he had to fight from the bottom of his guts and heart to win. He said he thought he and Hearns were both champions.

Hearns, who would not wear dark glasses until the next day, when the lumps he had received from Sugar Ray would start turning black-and-blue, had only praise for Leonard. They were both champions, he said, and one had to go, but he didn't plan to be gone for long. "Detroit," he promised his hometown fans, "I will return."

Already, people were talking about a rematch, for this had been an exciting fight. Not just exciting but one for the record books, one for history. It had been boxing at its very best. The same thing could not be said for the scoring, at least in the opinion of many. They found it unbelievable that all three judges had Hearns ahead on their scorecards going into the fourteenth round. The majority of sportswriters at ringside had scored the bout much closer, and some had Leonard slightly ahead. A few later wrote that Sugar Ray had not been up against one opponent but five—Hearns, the referee, and the three judges. Leonard's people agreed. If the fight had gone all 15 rounds without a knockout or a technical knockout, their man would have lost. That would have been hard to accept. Mike Trainer said he was convinced that Ray would never win a close decision because too many people in boxing resented him.

The Leonards were soon to feel somebody's resentment. Hardly had they returned to their hotel suite when an anonymous caller threatened to blow them up. They quickly relocated to another hotel, and nothing more was heard from the bomber. Nervously, they realized that they were likely targets for crazies, because Sugar Ray was so famous.

Hopefully more numerous than the crazies were the people who were just plain jealous, and there had to be a lot of them. At the age of 25, Sugar Ray Leonard had won more money in boxing than most of the previous champions combined. With the first Duran fight, he had set a world record for dollars earned in a single sports event. Now, having won more than $10 million in the fight against Hearns, he had broken his own record. He held not only the undisputed world welterweight title but the WBA junior middleweight title as well. That was quite a special position to enjoy. He was credited with almost single-handedly reviving the popularity not just of boxing in weight classes below heavyweight, but of boxing in general.

And finally, he seemed to have such a happy personal life. His wife was beautiful. His son was so photogenic and appealing that he was as responsible for the popularity of the Leonard Seven-Up commercials as his father was. He had a gorgeous home, proud parents, and a circle of loyal friends and business associates. With all that going for him, how could Ray Leonard escape being the object of jealousy?

Sugar Ray understood that he would have to deal with the jealousy of other people. He realized that some would watch his future fights hoping that he would be beaten soundly. They would get their chance to hope, for Sugar Ray Leonard had no intention of quitting now. He was "on a roll," as they say in dice games—winning and doing special things, like holding two titles at the same time. In a week, he would relinquish the WBA junior middleweight title, for WBA rules forbid the holding of two titles simultaneously, and now that he was the welterweight champion of the WBC *and* the WBA he had to abide by the rules of both organizations. But the fact that he had held these simultaneously will still go down in boxing history as something special.

And so will Sugar Ray. In part, he is responsible for the large number of talented young men who have entered boxing, inspired by his success. And, no matter what happens, when he quits, he will quit at the top. He has proven that although he was named for a singing star and nicknamed for a boxing star, he had what it takes to become a star on his own.

A few of the honors and trophies Sugar Ray has received.

INDEX

James Haskins, an avid fan of boxing, has taught in elementary and junior high schools and in colleges and universities in New York State and Indiana. Currently Professor of English at the University of Florida, he is the author of many books for young people, including biographies of Diana Ross and James Van DerZee.

As the Independent Bulletin of Chicago, Illinois, commented, "His basic message, both to his students and to his countless readers . . . is the timeless and timely message which says, 'You can!' "